RETURN
to
PLEASANT
Hill

RETURN to PLEASANT

Hill

Allen F. Harrod

To order additional copies of this book, contact:
Xlibris
1-888-795-4274
www.Xlibris.com
Orders@Xlibris.com
805646

Contents

ACKNOWLEDGEMENTS

M Y SPECIAL THANKS to the staff at Pleasant Hill, who in the tradition of the original Shakers, was always helpful while I did research there. In addition, these books by Edward Deming Andrews, *The Community Industries of the Shakers: The People Called Shakers, Shaker Furniture,* and *Work and Worship: The Economic Order of the Shakers;* James Archambeault, *The Gift of Pleasant Hill,* Thomas D. Clark, *Pleasant Hill and Its Shakers* and *Pleasant Hill in the Civil War; Thomas D. Clark and F. Gerakd Ham, Pleasant Hill and the Shakers;* Clarke Garrett, *Origins of the Shakers –From the Old World to the New;* Gerald F. Ham, *Shakerism In the Old West* and *Pleasant Hill Hill-A Century of Kentucky Shakerism (1805-1910):* Julia Neal, Stephen J. Stein, in his Masterful work, *The Shaker Experience in America, all* these provided factual insights into Shaker life and beliefs.

The main characters in the novel are fictitious, but limited Romances did blossom in all the Shaker communities across America. Historical Characters associated with the Shakers Society make their appearance in the book. I have tried to be faithful in representing lifestyle and beliefs accurately. The cover picture is provided by the Library of Congress photographer Lester Jones. It is the interior view of the Centre Family House from the second floor. Note the double stairwells-one for the men and one for the women. My thanks to Courtnie Morine for editing the book.

And finally, to my daughter Elizabeth Schulte who made valuable suggestions, always encouraged me, and formatted the book.

PREFACE

THIS BOOK IS a sequel to my previous book *Romance at Pleasant Hill*. Although a Preface usually contains a brief introduction to a present book, I think it would be helpful to do a brief review of the previous book.

Romance at Pleasant Hill begins with thirteen boys who were adopted from an orphanage in New Orleans by Trustee Micajah Burnett on a marketing trip of Shaker wares such as brooms, seeds, medical herbs and fruit preserves. Two of those boys, while given fictitious names David Matthews and Henry DeVoe became roommates and fast friends through life.

David worked on the Shaker Ferry below the village. There he met Captain Hillard Manning who became a devoted confidant. It was on the Ferry that David was introduced to the beautiful young Sarah Miles. The

Shakers were celibate and were forbidden to interact with the other sex, the female living in one side of the large house and the males another. Separate stairs led to their sleeping quarters and they were prohibited from conversation with people of the world-anyone that was not a Shaker.

But love finds a way. Secretly David leaves the Village and meets with Sarah and her father Thomas Miles. In time David leaves Pleasant Hill to work for Thomas Miles in his local grocery store and to be near Sarah. Winning the hearts of not only Sarah, but the affection of her parents, he proposes and marries Sarah. They moved to nearby Nicholasville where he works in a bank and she teaches English and Literature. Three children bless their family-Luke, Benjamin and Ruth. The story closes around the family fireplace.

Return to Pleasant Hill deals with the struggles to uncover David and Henry's past in New Orleans, returning to the declining Village of Pleasant, and the struggles of a couple's loss of a child, the temptation to violate sacred marriage vows, and the growing bond of love between a husband and wife.

CHAPTER ONE

TWO MEN FRESH from the Civil War knocked vigorously at the large oak door of the East Family Shaker House of Pleasant Hill. Oddly, one was dressed in a worn Union uniform and the other in a tattered Confederate uniform. It was difficult to call it a uniform, though, as it was ravaged far by war. Two holes stood out on the bloodstained coat; the sleeves and collar were frayed; the grey in the trousers was faded from wear and washing. They were brothers from Finchville, Kentucky, a small village outside Shelbyville, trying to get home. Miraculously, they had met up at Appomattox where, after four years of war, a weary General Robert E. Lee signed a formal surrender to Ulysses S. Grant at the Courthouse three days earlier on June 2, 1865. They had traveled from Virginia to Kentucky, selling their horses for food and board mid-way on their journey home. Walking for much of their journey, the pair was able to hitch rides on the back of sympathetic farmers' wagons along the way, often fed by strangers. As they traveled across the mountains of Eastern Kentucky, many grew suspicious of them and refused to be hospitable and take them in. However, the brothers had heard that the Shaker Village would provide food and a place to sleep for them.

"Our quarters are full," said an Elder of the Village, standing in the doorway, "but you can sleep in the loft of the cow barn if you'd like. As for food, give us some time, and you will have plenty to eat. They will be leftovers from our evening meal."

"That would be excellent; we are very hungry," said the Union soldier. "We haven't eaten in days." After a few minutes, roast wild turkey with stuffing, a large bowl of gravy, butter beans, beets, and several homemade sourdough biscuits were brought out. The brothers ate everything on their plates as the shared their war stories.

Their Shaker hosts had lots of questions about their war experiences: "How did one of you end up in the Union Army and the other in the Confederate? Where is Finchville? What are your names? What do you plan to do now that the war is over? Are both of your parents living? What does your father do for a living?" The questions seem never to end from the curious but pacifist Shakers.

"Bobby Roberts," said the older of the two men, extending his hand. "Randy Roberts," said the shorter young man in the tattered Confederate uniform. "Our father is deceased, died of a heart attack two years ago while we were away at war."

"Mom," said Bobby, "has been doing all she can to keep the farm up. We will be taking over the reigns as soon as we get home."

"Is there anything else you need?" asked Refus.

"No," said Bobby, "that meal was great," rubbing his stomach.

Rufus Bryant, Jr., Elder over the dairy barn, stood up, "I will show you to the hay loft. Sister Mary Cummings will get you some quilts. It is supposed to snow tonight. Breakfast will be served at 6 o'clock in the dining room. Men sit on the east side and women on the west."

"Mary Cummings, I thought I recognized you! Aren't you from Bagdad, Kentucky?" quizzed the man in the Union uniform.

She looked at him without acknowledging his question. It was not proper for a female Shaker to carry on a conversation with someone of the world. Elder Rufus answered for her. "Her husband dropped her and their two children off here three years ago. It seems he was interested in making money out West in the gold mines."

"Thanks for the meal and a place to sleep tonight. We would be glad to work for your hospitality," said Randy, standing to up brush the crumbs from his lap.

"That won't be necessary," said Elder Jones.

That night a snowstorm blew in from the east, covering the ground with six inches of snow. The brothers spent two more days and nights at the Shaker's table and in their barn loft. When the snow melted, Rufus brought a pair of slightly worn shoes for the Confederate soldier. His feet were almost totally bear from their journey. "I hope these fit," he said as he sat them down on the soft hay.

"I am sure they will be fine. With almost bare feet you can hardly complain."

"If they don't fit, we can find others," said Rufus, smiling.

When it came time to leave, they placed a few dollars in Confederate and Union bills on the knoll post of the East House along with a note of thanks. They were not the first and would not be the last soldier to arrive hungry at the door of the Shakers, but they would be the most courteous.

Later that month some Federal soldiers arrived, enjoyed a hardy meal, and took two of the best Shakers horses when they left. They were branded U.S. having been purchased from the government. But they had no bill of sale, so it was impossible to convince the soldiers otherwise, not that they wanted to be convinced to leave the horses if the Shakers had possessed such papers. Elder Rufus Jones wrote the Secretary of State and President Lincoln about the incident, and in two weeks two horses were delivered back to Pleasant Hill with apologies from both the Secretary of State and the President.

Over the next two years, transits, vagabonds, and rouge bands of former Confederate soldiers dropped in to pay their respects, eat a free meal, and steal whatever they could. Shakers stood watch from the top floor of the Center House day and night watching for strangers, protecting their possessions, hiding their horses in the woods and guarding their beef cattle.

Even though the War was over in most places, southern resistance continued during Reconstruction, which only lasted a little over ten years. Early on, President Lincoln refused to make abolition of slavery a part of the War. He feared such a move would alienate Border States that were still loyal to the Union. In 1863, Lincoln enacted the Emancipation Proclamation, freeing over 3 million slaves. Two years later, during a speech in Louisiana, he proposed that freed blacks and those that served in the military should be allowed to vote. Three days later John Wilkes Booth, an American actor, assassinated the President during a play at Ford's theater.

Most people did not consider Kentucky to be a Union State; however, there were some slave owners living in the state. Louisville had a strong slave trade, shipping many slaves South for sale, particularly New Orleans. Many Kentuckians sided with the Union army. Important figures in the state government demanded that the Union flag be flown over the Frankfort Capitol.

CHAPTER TWO

T HE CIVIL WAR formally ended in 1865, but strong tensions remained between the northern and southern states. Slavery topped this list of reasons even though reconstruction had been instituted three years earlier. Another lingering issue was state's rights. The power dynamic between an individual state and the Federal government was debated, and still is, for various reasons. A third issue that created tension was civil rights of freed slaves. The right to vote was made difficult for people of color through intimidation and the setting of unaffordable poll taxes. Additionally, the literacy rates among African Americans were quite low, making informed voting even more difficult. Kentucky voted not to withdraw from the Union, although divisions remained between many residents.

Reconstruction began sooner in Kentucky than in the more southern states. The Confederate army had moved out of Kentucky by 1862, freeing it from military rule. Peaceful attempts by both pro-Union and pro-Southerners began to reunite both factions. Churches, unified as brothers and sisters in Christ, sought to mend their differences. Soon, military authority of the North took over Kentucky. Yet, there was still resistance of those opposing their presence by those called the "Regulators" that met secretly. Ultimately, things begun to resolve and the state returned to some semblance of peaceful living.

Reconstruction staggered on as Andrew Johnson took the Presidency after the death of Lincoln. Despite his resistance, revolutionary changes took place in the government with African Americans winning seats in the House of Representatives and the Senate. During Reconstruction, the South's first federally funded public school began.

During a Sunday morning sermon at the Nicholasville Baptist Church, the pastor delivered a message on the freeing of the Children of Israel out of Egyptian bondage. He railed against the terribleness of slavery and impossibility of any Christian to support segregation, noting that such actions as separate water fountains, refusal of service at restaurants, and blocking their right to vote could not be tolerated. There were a few hearty amens from some in the congregation, others nodded approval, but some remained starkly silent. Being a new pastor to this congregation, he was unaware that one of his deacons owned a pharmacy that practiced segregation.

When a Chinese family purchased a grocery store and attended the Church, they received a cold reception from some of its members. Afterward, the Wong's received two anonymous letters expressing their displeasure with their presence in the church. The family never returned. If the pastor was unaware of the Southern sympathies of some his church members, he was soon to discover the anger his biblical sermon stirred up. Shortly after the sermon, a special deacons meeting was called. Twelve deacons and the pastor crowded into the meeting room. Tension was high.

The chairman of deacons cleared his throat as he turned to the pastor, "I suppose you know why this meeting was called."

Surprised, "Actually, I don't," responded the pastor sensing that he might be the reason. "Suppose you tell me Marvin."

"Well," looking around the room for support, "there are several people unhappy with your slavery comments during your morning sermon two weeks ago."

"Is that right?" said the pastor. "Just what did I say that they didn't like?" his voice tightening.

The chairman moved to the edge of his seat as he nervously said, "I am afraid that we might lose them if you don't go to some of our members and apologize."

"Who are these people?"

"I can't say."

Another of the deacons visibly unhappy with the direction of the meeting challenged the chairman, "Marvin, if you won't tell us who they are, how is the pastor going to go to them?"

"Now, I didn't say I agreed with them, but I am chairman of the deacons," He said defensively.

"Then you should have supported the pastor and protected him," injected Deacon John Marshall.

David, another deacon, had been quiet as he listed to the charges. Now he was on his feet, "It seems to me that we haven't addressed the proper question: Did the pastor preach what is true? If he did, and I believe he did, these people who are unhappy with his remarks need to take a long look at their attitudes concerning people of color." Several deacons nodded in agreement. "It is more than likely that Jesus had a tanned skin from being out in the Palestine sun so much. As far as I understand, according to the Bible, He rode into Jerusalem on a borrowed donkey." Several chuckled. "Frankly, if Jesus would not be welcome because of his brown skin in our church, I really don't know if I want to continue as a member here." It grew quieter as David sat down. Bill Miller, long time member and deacon in the church, stood up. Choosing his words carefully, "Brothers, David has expressed my sympathy exactly." The Chairman, his face red, said nervously, "I will take care of this matter. Do I hear a motion that we adjourn?" Several of the deacons spoke at the same time calling for adjournment. Chairman Frank Scoggins shook the pastor's hand fiercely apologizing for not defending him. "It is all right, Frank. I have an eraser on the end of my pencil. I am sure you will take care of the matter."

The meeting closed without a further word as the men dispersed to their carriages.

The next day, Pastor Ken Butler dropped by the bank to acknowledge his appreciation for David's stand in deacon's meeting. "It was just the right thing to do pastor," David replied. They shook hands and as the pastor responded, "I hope you never consider leaving our church David. I value your support."

The issue was never mentioned in a formal church meeting again, but the pharmacy owner and his wife moved their membership to different church. After two months, they moved their membership again to a small, part-time church out in the country.

CHAPTER THREE

O UT IN THE distance, on May 15, 1876, the lonesome sound of the L&N locomotive grew louder as it approached the Lexington Railroad Station, tooting its horn before approaching Country Crossings. Numerous people from all walks of life waited patiently on the landing, in the brisk air, as the engine slowed in its approach, grinding its massive wheels to a screeching halt as it released steam from the cylinders. Lexington was a booming town with some of the last L&N rails recently competed.

The buggy of Thomas Miles waited; the pair of horses chomped the grassy knoll while the passengers chatted in the cool morning air. The horses shifted nervously as steam was released from the train's pressure value.

David hugged and kissed Sarah as he and Henry prepared to board the train. "I hope you and Henry discover more about your families. Have a great time! Don't eat too much Cajun food."

"Thanks for bringing us to train," said David, extending his hand. Thomas Miles pulled him close, kissing him on the cheek. "Be careful son! New Orleans is a rough place with a large criminal element. Watch after him Henry."

David was stunned. He had never known his father-in-law to be affectionate before. "I will Dad!"

The conductor led David and Henry to their seats. They were comfortable enough for the first few hours. The date March 6, 1867 stood out in bold letters on the *Lexington Statesman* newspaper that David held up as he read the business section. Then, turning to the local section, his eye caught a headline: "Jessie James Gang Robs Russellville, Kentucky Bank." "Did you see this article about the bank robbery at Russellville a few days ago?" David asked, holding his paper forward for Henry to see.

"No, I haven't read the newspaper today. Was anyone hurt?"

"According to the report, the President of the bank was killed when he tried to wrestle a gun from one of the gang members."

David returned to his paper, "Looks like Nicholasville is going to get about six inches of rain while we are gone."

"Wow! That ought to slow the farmer's down." Turning back to the window, Henry watched intently as farmers gathered in their crops of hay and corn before the night closed them down.

"Look at this Henry," David said excitedly, "The U.S. buys Alaska from Russia for $7,209.00."

"Incredible! Guess I won't have to read the paper tonight; I am getting it with commentary first-hand. Any other breaking news?"

David smiled.

A toddler climbed down out of his seat while his mother changed the diaper on his infant brother. He laughed and giggled as he ran down the isle of the train.

As he passed David snatched him up and began to play with him. His mother quickly pinned her infant's diaper and laid him on the seat as she jumped up and ran down the aisle. "Joey," she called in broken English.

"Not to worry, I have him," called David holding him up for her to see.

"I am very sorry," she said as she approached.

"No problem, I have children of my own. Let me help you with him for a while. I see that you have another little one to take care of."

Hesitating, she agreed. "If he becomes a problem bring him back to me," she said with a French accent.

David assured her that he would be no problem. He played pattycake and other two-year-old games with him until he fell asleep on his chest.

"Go on to your berth," said David, "I will be along shortly."

After a while David fell asleep also. Gently, a touch on his shoulder awakened him. Joey's mother reached out. "Thank you," she said tenderly taking him into her arms.

"I enjoyed every minute of it," he said softly. "I have two sons and a daughter of my own."

"That was a kind thing for you to do," whispered Henry as David climbed into the bunk above him.

The next morning David looked up the aisle in search of the mother and her children, but the seats they had occupied were empty. *Probably got off at one of the stops in the night.*

After transferring from the Louisville & Nashville to the New Orleans & Chattanooga train they finally arrived in New Orleans at 11:25 a.m., secured their bags, and stepped out into the crisp morning air of Loyola Avenue.

"Where do we go from here?" asked Henry as he looked up and down the street.

"I guess we try to find Saint Jerome's Orphanage. Maybe they can give us some information on our families. A policeman or a Catholic Church ought to be able to give us an address."

"What about the ticket office here at the station they may know where it is?"

"Good idea," said David.

An elderly man sitting on a bench overheard their conversation. "You are looking for St. Jerome Boys Orphanage?"

"Yes, sir. Do you know where it is located?" Henry inquired. "We lived there for several years before we were taken to a Shaker Village in Pleasant Hill, Kentucky."

"Kentucky? You fellows are a long way from home," chuckled the elderly man. "As for St. Jerome, I will be passing by there in about thirty minutes. My son is on the way to pick me up. I just arrived from Baton Rouge, where my daughter and husband live. Been visiting them for a month, since my wife died. If you want to wait a bit, we can give you a ride. In fact, there comes my son now."

"That would be great Mr., say, what is your name if you have no objection to my asking," inquired David.

"Not at all. It is Antoine Boucher. The first name is French meaning wealthy or rich and the surname is Spanish meaning butcher. My father was one of the revolutionaries who sought to take New Orleans back from the Spanish in 1768. The attempt failed a year later when our leaders were captured; five of them sent to a prison in Cuba and five were executed. My father, along with some others, was freed on the promise that they would give their allegiance to the Spanish government, which they did. In gratitude, my father changed his surname, giving me a Spanish name when I was born. That is a bit of my history. I must tell you more. Where are you staying here in New Orleans?"

"Well, we haven't made arrangements yet. We just arrived," admitted David. "We are here to find out something about our family background. We were placed in the St. Jerome Orphanage during the cholera epidemic when our parents died."

"Perfect, you can stay at my house. We have several extra rooms, and you will to be our guests."

"We couldn't possibly put you out."

"I insist! My son and I live there alone. It would be a privilege to have you. Son, these two gentlemen are our guests for a few days. Please take their baggage."

"Certainly, Dad! My name is Bernard," extending his hand, "things get terribly dull around our big house since my mother died, and I must warn you that we are not the greatest chefs."

"I am sure it will be fine. My name is David Matthews, and this is Henry DeVoe. Henry is a doctor in Nicholasville, Kentucky and I work in a bank there. As we told your father, we were once residents of St. Jerome Orphanage before we were taken to a Shaker Village in Pleasant Hill, Kentucky, which is a long story we can share with you later."

Henry looked at David and nodded. "We can pay for our board."

"Not at all. You will pay nothing. It will be our pleasure," Antoine said in a clipped French tone. "We will help you in your search for your ancestry. Tomorrow, we will take you to the orphanage, if that is all right?"

"That would be perfect, but I just feel we are imposing on your hospitality," David replied. "You will bless us with your presence," insisted Antoine. "I hope the animals in our house will not bother you. We have two German Shepherds that have pretty much run of the house. They have a ferocious bark, but they wouldn't harm a flea."

"We both have dogs," said Henry. "We love animals. That is another part of our story. The Shakers never allowed dogs at the Village except the one owned by our dairy farmer– a Collie for herding."

"Well, let's get going. Bernard, we must take them to Jane's for dinner, the best Cajon cuisine restaurant in the city."

"Only, if you let us have the bill," said Henry.

"No promises! We shall see. Maybe, we will flip for it," Antoine, laughing stated. Soon, they pulled up before an antiquated, two-story brick building.

A young waitress seated the men near a window overlooking Lake Pontchartrain. Fishing boats and pleasure vessels filled the bay. "What a terrific view," marveled Henry as he scooted down the bench.

"Do you like fish?" asked Antoine.

David looked at Henry; they both nodded yes.

You can look at the menu, but I suggest the fish platter starting with crawfish bisque and jambalaya made with kielbasa sausage and shrimp over dirty rice, and stuffed red fish, with black-eyed peas and cheddar potatoes as a side."

"Sounds great! I am hungrier than a bear."

Antoine entertained the group with stories about early New Orleans. After the main course the waitress came back and asked, "Would you like our special Jane's Pecan Buttermilk Pie?"

"Oh, I don't know," said David pushing back from the table.

"You must at least try a small piece," said Antoine, "it is out of this world."

"Well, maybe David and I can half a piece," concluded Henry. "We have had a big meal already."

"You must have a whole piece," insisted Antoine as he motioned to the waitress for the check.

David reached up to take the bill. "Sorry, sir. Sheriff Boucher has already asked for the bill."

"It is the least we can do," insisted David, "so you are the Sheriff of New Orleans?"

Shaking his hand downward Antoine said in Spanish "De Nada! It is nothing! I was Sheriff for thirteen years, but I retired two years ago. People still address me as Sheriff."

Antoine sang the French love song "L Hymne A L'amour" in his high tenor voice all the way home. Loud barks came from the inside as they approached the grand house. "Not to worry, they won't hurt you," said Antoine. Lifting their bags from the buggy, he pointed toward the house.

"Can we help with unhitching the horses?"

"It is no problem," called Bernard. "I will have to show you my buggy repair shop tomorrow. That is my profession."

Antoine placed a large brass key in the door lock, turned it, and pushed it open. "Now Hans and Fritz," addressing the dogs, "these are our guests and you must be polite to them." The dogs cocked their heads to the side as if they understood his instruction, whimpering as the men entered. David reached down for them to smell his hand and Henry did likewise. "You must be exhausted. I will show you to your room." Up the long stairs they followed Antoine to a room with two bunk beds. "This used to be Bernard and Brandon's room, Brandon was a twin son who drowned while swimming in a lake. He was only fifteen at the time."

"I am very sorry," said Henry, "the same thing almost happened to me when I was near his age. I dove into a new lake and hit a stump hidden below the water. Had David not rescued me I would not be here today."

"I must warn you that Hans and Fritz may claw on the door for you to let them in. If you open it, they will only sleep at the end of your beds."

"I assure you they will be no problems to us," said David.

"Breakfast will be served when you are up and dressed. I get up early, but you may sleep in as long as you like. Goodnight, gentlemen, and have a good rest," he bade them, leaving the door ajar. Soon after Fritz and Hans entered taking their place at the end of the beds, but they left when they heard Antoine downstairs the next morning.

The smell of bacon and eggs frying drifted up from the kitchen, along with Antoine's tenor voice singing "La Mer" in English.

"David and Henry, did you sleep well?" asked Bernard as they entered the kitchen. "I hope Fritz and Hans did not keep you awake. They can be pests."

"Like a rock," offered Henry.

"One of them laid his head on my chest for a few minutes and then took his place at the end of the bed as you said, but he was no problem."

"That would have been Fritz, he was my twin brother Brandon's dog."

Along with a delightful breakfast of bacon, eggs, and grits, Antoine served up intriguing stories about his early days as sheriff of New Orleans. "It was a rough and rugged city in those days. It still has a large criminal population"

"We should get to the orphanage by ten o'clock. That will give them time for chapel. Does that sound all right? I will accompany you for any translation problems," advised Antoine. "Cajun can be a little difficult."

"Are we far from the orphanage?" Henry inquired.

"Actually, it is only six blocks away."

"Perfect! We can walk"

"We may need the buggy later, so it will be best to take it with us."

CHAPTER FOUR

T HE SUN WAS shining brightly, and the rain had ceased. Children were playing in the yard as they pulled up the drive of the large grey rock building. Pink credendum's spread their large leaves, decorating the corners of the building. Tropical blue hibiscus flowered the stone steps entering the building. The walks going up to the building were lined appropriately with angel trumpets on one side and bird of paradise on the other. The Persian shield scattered over the yard provided a sweet fragrance that delighted the nostrils.

"I remember this building faintly, maybe more will come back to me," observed David, as they stood before the large, double-glass, wooden doors. Henry reached for the door hanger, but his hand froze. He could see a Catholic nun smiling back from inside the hall. Pulling the doors open she greeted them with an invitation to enter. She was too young for Henry and David to remember her, not that they would anyway. "I am Sister Teresa, can I help you?" she smiled.

"We lived here," answered David, "nine years ago. We would like to see if you have any information about our parents."

"You would need to see Sister Angelia. She in charge of the records, and was here then," she explained, ushering them down the long hall to a room where an elderly nun was sitting at a desk. "Sister, these gentlemen were residents here nine years ago and they would like to talk to you."

"Please, come in." Recognizing Antoine, she rose from her chair. "Are these two young men in trouble Sherriff?"

"No, not at all. They are guests in my home," he said laughing loudly.

"How can I help you gentlemen?"

"Sister Angelia, I am David Matthews, and this is Henry DeVoe. Nine years ago, Elder Micajah Burnett, from Pleasant Hill Shaker Village in Kentucky visited here and took thirteen of your boys, including Henry and me back with him to Kentucky." He paused waiting for a response.

The sister hesitated for a moment as if wondering if she should acknowledge the event. "Yes, I do remember that, and I remember both of you. Those were difficult days for the orphanage, and we were overcrowded. It was a hard decision, but it had to be made. You have grown up into fine looking young men."

"And I remember you. You were very kind to us while we were here. Henry and I no longer live at the Shaker Village. We are both married and have children. We live in Nicholasville, Kentucky where Henry is a medical doctor and I am a bank employee. We would like to find out more about our families and thought you may be able to help us." The fragrance from the lavender bouquet of purple carnations and chrysanthemums sitting on her desk were about to lose their delightful smell.

"I am not sure that we have any more information than you already know, and if we did, I am not permitted to reveal it. I am sorry that you traveled so far, I cannot be of any more assistance to you."

David started to speak when Antoine stepped up. "David and Henry, if you could wait out in the hall, I would like to speak to Sister Angelia."

Henry looked at David with raised eyebrows as they exited the room. Outside they overheard an intense discussion. The Sister said, "But you are no longer the acting Sherriff." In a forceful voice Antoine insisted that there was no reason that he should not see the records, "after all they are twenty-one years old now. They have a right to know about their parents. In the name of all that is holy you cannot send them home without sharing whatever information you have." There was a silence and after a while Antoine came out the door smiling. In his hand were some copies of files.

"Did you find anything?" asked David. "I didn't know who was going to win that debate, you or the Sister."

"When you have been Sherriff as long as I have, you can collect a few favors. I reminded her that I gave her brother a break, at her request, when he was charged with assault several years back. Facts sometimes are handy," he declared with a grin. "Out of respect for the Sister, though, we must wait until we are away from the orphanage before looking at what we have. It is not a great deal, but it may lead up to a better source."

"Of course," agreed Henry, grinning. "It is the least we can do for her volunteer help."

"Giddy up girls," the Sherriff commanded, tapping the brown horses lightly on the back. They rode down the street to a boat dock off Lake Pontchartrain. The water lapped against the shore in a rhythmic manner. "According to my agreement with the Sister, I cannot give the file to you directly, but I can share it with you as a law official," clearing his throat and smiling sheepishly. "We will start with David. Your parents were Julian and Fanny Matthews and they lived on 150 Alain Callendor Street, in a duplex house they shared with your father's sister Natalia Lysenko. She was never married, and still lives in the house. I knew both of your parents." David's mind danced with excitement. They pulled up to the yellow house with diamond cornice overhanging the split porch. The shutters were green, and the doors were orange. Twin metal railings lined each side door of the shotgun house. On the black mailbox was the name Lysenko.

The door slowly cracked opened as a low voice asked, "Who is it?" David cleared his throat. "It is David Matthews I think I am related to you."

The door swung open, as Natalia, unlocked the metal security gate leading into the house. She began to cry and say something in Russian, grabbing the sides of her face. "It cannot be, it cannot be," she cried softly, throwing her arms around his neck, kissing him on both cheeks. She continued for a while until she noticed Antoine and Henry. "Oh, I am sorry, please come in, please come in. Sit down. You are David, Julian and Fanny's boy?" Withdrawing the scarf from around her neck she dabbed her watery eyes. "Yes, you have your father's eyes and mother's dimples." She stood, "I must make some café. I have some fresh Praline cookies."

David spoke as she left the room, "It is not necessary." Antoine stretched out his hand rejecting his words, "In New Orleans, you never refuse an offer of hospitality in a home." "We will wait!" offered David.

She returned a few minutes later with a carafe of coffee and a silver tray of pecan cookies. "This tray was your mother's. It was brought here from the Netherlands, and now it will be yours," she said sitting across from David. "Are you in trouble? Why is Sherriff Boucher here? And, who is this other fine-looking young man with you?"

"Well, Aunt Natalia, Henry was in the orphanage with me when we were taken to Kentucky. And, we met Sherriff Boucher at the train station where he graciously took us into his home and helped us locate you."

"I know you must have a hundred questions," she said squeezing David's hand, "but let me begin by telling you how you ended up in the orphanage. When your father and mother died, I came down with cholera and somehow survived. During my sickness the police came and took you away to the orphanage. It was awhile before I found out where you were. When I was released from the hospital, I visited the orphanage to bring you home with me, but they would not allow me to see you. I left your father's gold watch and your parents' names on a piece of paper. The next time I visited the orphanage they still refused to let me see you. I don't suppose they gave the watch to you?" Not waiting for an answer, she continued, "I went back many times, but they still refused to allow me to see you. I would walk past the orphanage hoping to see you playing in the yard, but you were never there. The last time I visited they said you had been adopted by someone from another state, but they wouldn't say where." She began to cry again, and then wiping her eyes, "I had to sell almost everything of your parents for their funerals. I saved a few things which I have kept for you should you ever return. I had almost given up hope of ever finding you!"

She went over to a large walnut chifforobe where she retrieved a box with two tintype pictures and a purple necklace.

David pulled the watch from his pocket and showed it to his Aunt. "This watch is part of my miracle story and Henrys."

"Yes, that was your father's watch." She pulled out a picture of his parents sitting on chairs in front of the house; hanging from a gold fob in his vest pocket was the watch. She retrieved another picture from the Honest Scrap tobacco tin. "This picture was made by a traveling photographer at the funeral of your parents. Now, they are yours," passing them to him.

David studied the second one for a time, then asked, "Why are there two boys standing beside their caskets?"

"Why, that is your older brother Jacob. He was taken to the orphanage and adopted soon after. They said by a nice, young Jewish couple."

"An older brother! So that is who is standing beside me, in front of a casket, in my dreams. All this time I thought it was Henry. That is why I couldn't figure the dream out."

There was no color to the picture, but now he knew what his parents really looked like.

"There is one question I have, why is your name different from my father's since you were never married?"

"The Jews were greatly persecuted in Russia under Czar Nicholas, who sought to destroy them. Your grandparents lived in Zhitomir, one of the Pale Settlements."

"The Pale Settlement?"

"That was an area where Jews in Russia were allowed to live in certain cities," she hesitated. "One day, while your father and I were away from the city visiting friends a mob descended on our town and killed many people, including your grandparents and our uncle Joshua. He was unmarried and lived with them. When we came home, the house and everything in it was burned to the ground. We never saw our parents or brother again. We were told they were in the house when it was set on fire."

"But why?" David asked.

"Because we were Jews! Julian and I moved to a small town next to the Baltic Sea, where we lived with an uncle and aunt, working as fishermen to raise money to escape to England. Later, we were able to come to America. After living in New York for thirteen months where your father worked with a fishing fleet, we moved to Orleans. Your father met and married your mother Natalia Gonwa here. She was from the Netherlands. A few years later he bought this house. After their death, I have lived here, renting out the other side to pay the mortgage. Your father changed his name to the American name of Matthews, fearing he might be persecuted here. His original last name was Lysenko, as is mine."

David stood up. "Aunt Natalia, we must go now. We are also trying to find out something about Henry's parents. I will contact you tomorrow for another visit because I want to know more about my parents and grandparents."

She took David by the arm and walked him to the door, "You won't forget me, will you?"

"Of course not. I will be back tomorrow or the next day. You must write all this down for me. When we return to Kentucky, I will make plans for you to come and visit us for a long stay. There you can meet your nephews and niece."

"Let me know ahead of time of when you will return and I will cook a good meal for you, Antoine, and Henry. It will be a common Jewish dinner of stuffed cabbage with ground beef, rice, and yellow potatoes on the side. It will be covered with a rich tomato sauce made of chopped apples, onions, tomatoes, brown sugar, lemon juice, a little cider, and a finely grated lemon. It was your father's favorite dish. Yes, that is what we shall have."

"I will have some more things that I have saved for you that belonged to your parents. They have been stored in a hall closet awaiting your arrival."

Standing, David turned to Antoine. "Are you sure we are not taking too much of your time? It has been an eventful day."

"None sense. I have nothing but time."

They said goodbye and departed, promising to return on Wednesday at ten o'clock. Tears welled in Natalia's eyes as she kissed David on the cheek and hugged him for a final time before he left. David did the same.

As they climbed into the buggy Antoine pulled a yellow sheet from his pocket, "Henry, I am afraid we have little information on your family. Sister Angelia did tell me, off the record, of an incident two weeks after you were brought to the orphanage. She heard that you father was killed while trying to apprehend a robber who attacked an elderly couple. It all happened a block from the orphanage. The wife of the man, who was shot, was saved by your father's heroic act. He was thought to be on his way to the orphanage. A man who viewed the incident and tried to help your father told Sister Angelia that he kept looking toward the orphanage. His last words were, 'My boy, the orphanage. I must take him home.'"

Tears welled up in Henry's eyes, "So he didn't abandon me. All these years I thought he had forgotten me. Was there anything else you learned about my father?" he urged.

"The file didn't say anything about your mother."

"My father told me before taking me to orphanage that my mother had left him for another man. Somehow I remember sitting on the rock wall outside the orphanage before he took me in and promising he would be back to get me." Henry turned away wiping his eyes. Finally, he regained his composure. "David, I was thinking while we visited your Aunt, that we ought to contact some Jewish Synagogues tomorrow. Maybe the Rabbi could tell us something about your brother."

David put his arm around Henry. "You are always thinking of others, Henry. I wish we had more information on your father."

"There is one more thing the Sister told me your father's full name was Henry Anthony DeVoe."

"That would make me a junior," announced Henry excitedly. He was quiet and pensive the rest of the way home while David and Antoine chatted about the history of New Orleans.

CHAPTER FIVE

"**D**O YOU THINK the Rabbi will see us?" asked David. "You can't refuse a Sherriff," declared Antoine, laughing as he cracked the reigns over the horses back. "Getty up, Sue. Getty up Sarah." There is a Jewish Temple over on Carondelet Street. It is called Dispersed of Judah, but I think we will give my friend Rabbi James Gutheim a visit first at the Gates of Mercy Temple. It is over on Rampart, between Conti and Saint Louis streets. I know him best. And I have some uncollected favors there," he said sheepishly.

"So, I guess he had a member who got in trouble that you helped out?" asked Henry with a chuckle.

"More than one. One man was a very important leader in the community got into a brawl with a neighbor over some woodcuttings left on his yard that his neighbor refused to move. They got into a tussle and the Jewish guy ended breaking some of the man's ribs. Anyway, we are here! The Rabbi lives next door to the synagogue."

The Sheriff gave a forceful knock on the door. Soon footsteps were heard in the long hall of the antiquated brown house. The door swung open and a broad shouldered, baldheaded Rabbi Gutheim appeared in the door. "Well, if it isn't my old friend Antoine. Come in! Come in!" looking over David and Henry, "Now these are not two of my young men, so I won't need your help."

"No, we aren't here because there is trouble. We are here for information."

"Sit down! Would you like a glass of wine?"

"Not for me," said David, as Henry held up his hand of refusal.

"Well, I won't turn you down Rabbi."

As he handed the glass to Antoine, he said, "Now, we have known each other too long for titles. It is James."

"We are looking for perhaps a member of your congregation by the last name of Lysenko. His name may have been changed to something else."

"Lysenko?" scratching his bald head.

"He was adopted into a Jewish family about..." Antoine hesitated.

"Twelve years ago," David chimed in.

"His father was Julian Matthews, a fisherman located over on at the wharf. He and his wife died of the cholera epidemic some years back. David, was placed in Saint Jerome and his brother was adopted by a Jewish couple."

"Julian Matthews, I knew your mother and father well. I bought fish from your father regularly and occasionally went fishing with him. He had a Jewish heritage and loved to tell Jewish jokes. His favorite was 'How was copper wire invented? By two Jews fighting over a copper penny," he said, slapping his knee.

David smiled, looked at Henry, wondering if he should laugh out loud.

"Yes, Julian was a great friend. Now, as to your brother Jacob, he was adopted by Simon and Batia, Hebrew variant of Bathia, Einhorn. Simon called her Betty. They could not have children and adopted Jacob and planned to adopt you later, but when they returned to the orphanage you were gone. They moved to Baton Rouge a few years back, but Jacob lives here. In fact, he has a jewelry business downtown. He is married and has a son. Six years ago, before he was married, he changed his name back to Lysenko. David, your father was a very fine man, honest, kind, and strong. Your mother was a very beautiful woman. I can see their features in you. You have your mother's black hair and dark brown eyes. You have your father's strong shoulders. They would be very proud of you carrying on the Jewish tradition."

"Rabbi Gutheim, I am a Christian."

"Well, fine," he asserted, "Knowing your parents as I did, I know they would be proud of you as a Christian. Your mother was Hebrew Christian, from the Netherlands.

"Yes sir, I have been told that," David expressed warmly, "and I appreciate your help and time today," he added as he stood to leave. They all shook hands and left.

Outside, David said, "Antoine, we are scheduled to leave on the train back to Nicholasville Wednesday afternoon. Do you think we could make a visit today at my brother's store downtown?"

"Of course, let's not waste time. It has certainly been an eventful day."

"We couldn't have done it without your help. God placed you in our path."

As they pulled up before the jewelry store David turned to Antoine and Henry, "I have not the slightest idea of what to say!'

"God will tell you," offered Henry.

"You will know," added Antoine.

David waited until his brother's customers finished their business. Jacob turned to David standing at the end of the counter and said, "Do I know you? You look familiar!"

"Hello, Jacob. I am David, your brother."

His brother broke into tears as he made his way from the back of the counter throwing his long arms around him. "I knew someday I would see you again," he sobbed. He dropped his arms, moved to the front door, turned the "Closed" sign over, and pulled the shade, then turned back to David.

"Jacob, this is my new friend, Sherriff Boucher, and my best friend Henry DeVoe. Henry and I were in the orphanage together and later taken to the Shaker Village in Kentucky. When we rolled in on the train, I had no idea I had a brother. Until, Aunt Natalia showed me a picture of us standing together before our parents' coffins."

"You must let me take you all out to dinner tonight. We will talk of times that were and times that should have been," announced Jacob. "You must meet my wife Amy and my son, Isaiah. I finish up here around 5 o'clock. Could you meet us around 6? That will give me time to pick up Aunt Natalia. We will go downtown to nice restaurant overlooking the bay. It is known for it's delightful…"

"Cajun cuisine," the trio answered in unison as they broke out into a loud laughter.

"You know the restaurant?" Jacob asked with a curious look on his face.

"We ate there last evening," said Antoine. "Anyway, it is not necessary that I join you. It is a family thing."

"I won't hear of it. You and your family must join us, but we will find another restaurant. I insist. What about Vincent's on St. Charles Avenue?"

"Sounds excellent. We will meet you there at six o'clock."

Later at dinner, David was seated between Natalia and Jacob. He had many questions about his father and mother that Jacob could answer. They talked on and on about their parents, life growing up and their future, until the restaurant owner said, "I am sorry, but it is time to close." Reluctantly, they all agreed and returned to their buggies. Ncouldn't stop patting David on the arm, and kissing his cheek, as Jacob took turns hugging him tightly promising to bring Natalia to Kentucky for a visit.

Bernard had a prior commitment with a young lady. Antoine, on the way home, sitting next to Henry, told exciting stories of capturing big-time criminal members of the French Quarter such as Marie Landnu, spiritualist that cut off chicken heads and danced around a burning fire or Delphine La Laurie, who tortured, mutilated and murdered her black slaves. "The spirits of these criminals are said to haunt the French Quarters today," insisted Antoine.

The next day, after a long visit at Natalia's little duplex, Jacob and Natalia stood at the railroad departure platform as David and Henry prepared to board the train. Natalia placed the tin box in David's hands.

The box contained items that had belonged to his mother and father; a well-worn pocket knife, a string of genuine pearls, two decorative hair pens, a red-rhinestone brooch, a small silver platter, a favorite fishing lure, a man's silver belt buckle with the initials J.L. and a third tintype picture of the family when David was around five years old. *The picture had to have been taken just before the cholera epidemic* he thought. He was holding the hand of his father and Jacob stood beside his mother holding her hand. Tears welled up in his eyes as he examined each item. He tried not to cry, but it was beyond what he could control. A lady across the aisle from him, sensing the situation, handed him a handkerchief. She apparently figured out what was happening. David dabbed his eyes and offered it back to the lady, but she smiled and closed his hand around it. He thanked her for the kindness. She nodded. Inside the larger box was a smaller one with a string around it. It was Natalia's wonderful pecan cookies. He handed the lady the box and she smiled as she took one. Henry took two and passed them back.

The return trip was long. Henry slept most of the way. David laid awake most of the night, thinking about his parents. The train rolled into Lexington around midnight. Thomas Miles waited, wrapped in a large blanket to ward off the cold. The snow dusted in his gray hair formally announced winter's arrival. When they finally reached Nicholasville the streets were decorated for Christmas. Long boughs of evergreen hung from lamppost. Large Christmas balls and ornaments hung from fences and store doors.

After dropping Henry off at his house, the buggy turned down Locust Street. The kerosene lamps were burning brightly in the window of the yellow brick home. Standing in the front room waiting was his mother-in-law Frances with Sarah beside her. He had so much to tell them, bit it would have to wait until tomorrow.

CHAPTER SIX

THREE WEEKS AFTER their return, in the shinny mailbox at the Matthews home, a letter and a yellow telegraph awaited pick-up. Both the letter and the telegraph were addressed to Mr. David Matthews, 113 Chestnut Drive, Nicholasville, Kentucky– their former address. This old address was marked out and the correct address, 1043 Heathcliff St., was added. *That is odd thought Sarah. I understand that Jim, our mailman could have corrected the letter, but who changed the address on the telegraph?* Both items had the same return address in a beautiful handwriting, of Natalie Lysenko, 13 Water Street, New Orleans, Louisiana.

The Matthew's house was a chocolate brown, two-story, brick with a small wood in back. A large fireplace adorned the living room that opened at the other side into the spacious kitchen. David called it his earthly haven of rest. He often watched varied wildlife out his study window: deer, fox, a bobcat, rabbits, and a ground hog they called Grumpy. Birds of all types gathered in the trees next to the house waiting their turn at the feeders, one filled with Sunflower seed for Cardinals, the state bird, and the other feeder filled with a sundry of seeds to attract smaller birds.

Sarah placed the stained letter and the telegraph on the Shaker walnut table in the hallway so David would see it when he returned from work. *Was the letter soiled from drops of rain or were they human teardrops?* She wondered.

Reading the return address, David quickly ran his finger down the envelope. It was indeed from his Aunt Natalia, informing him that she would be taking the train to see them in three weeks, noting the time of her arrival.

Once the weeks passed, they found themselves waiting as the locomotive rolled down the rain-drenched track. Natalia was weeping as she exited the train. Clutched in her hand was a yellow piece of paper on which she had recorded events, stories, and personality traits of David's mother and father–things totally unknown by him. Each evening after dinner they would sit around the fireplace as Aunt Natalia unfolded the yellow piece of paper to share. She began, "These are things that I remember about your parents. The first thing I remember about your father was that he was a generous person, always helping others, especially less fortunate people. When hungry people came to his boat, he always gave them fish and sometimes to women he gave money. Many of them were present at your parent's funeral."

"There was one woman that I particularly remember. Her name was Isabel Sledge. Her husband had died unexpectedly leaving her to raise five small children. She had a limited education. One day she showed up at your father's boat with a strange request. She asked for a basket of fish on credit that she could peddle from door to door, promising to pay for the fish when she sold them. Good for her word the next morning, she showed up at the boat with the payment and purchased a second basket that day. But not only did she pay your father for the fish, she built a very profitable business putting her children through high school and some through college."

"One evening she came to your father's boat with a story about her recent conversion to Christ and how she wanted to start tithing to her church. After that your father would always throw in some extra fish and say, 'These are for your tithe.' Your parents were guests in her home for several nice evening meals, sitting around the table and talking about events of the day in social and political life. Your father was an avowed Republican and so was Isabel."

"Your father was a religious man, not in the traditional sense that he attended synagogue regularly, but in reading a well-worn copy of the Bible, both the New and Old Testaments, that Isabel had given him. A month before they died, they had begun to attend a little Baptist Church near their home; they spoke of their intention of joining the congregation and becoming baptized."

"I am going to be baptized when I understand what it means to be a believer. Isn't that right, Papa?" offered Ruth. David smiled and nodded. Benjamin sat quietly in his chair listening to the conversation.

Natalie turned the paper over, "Your father was an honest man. When he gave his word, he kept it. He had three things he said over and over: 'Keep your word. If you can't keep it go to the person and explain why. Speak to everyone you meet, and pay your bills.'"

"Now about your Mother. She was a very modest person. She would never undress before even other females in the family. She had long black hair that was often rolled up in a bun on the back of her head, a petite little woman, very private. Beside working long hours at the garment factory, she had a little sewing business on the side. When your Father was out to sea fishing, she would sew late into the night."

Natalie paused, folding the paper, "I will tell you more about her tomorrow night. It is getting late."

"Tell us more, tomorrow is Saturday, and we don't have to go to school," begged Ruth.

"Well, one more thing tonight and tomorrow night I will tell you more about your grandmother. She was a wonderful cook. She could make corn bread that would melt in your mouth. Your grandfather looked forward to getting home from the boat because he knew a great meal awaited him. She cooked all kinds of seafood jambalaya, gumbo, and stuffed shrimp. One of your father's favorites was stuffed cabbage rolls. One of my favorites was a Cuban dish. It was chicken legs marinated in garlic sauce. She often made squash casserole. It was out of this world, so good."

"What are some other things she cooked?" asked Sarah.

"Country ham, the most delicious corn... Julian was a Jew, but he didn't follow the dietary laws. She could make butter beans that would melt in your mouth. She often whipped up a blackberry cobbler for him, his favorite dessert." Natalie was now looking across the room as if she saw Fannie standing in the kitchen over a wood stove. She was reliving the experiences of yester year. "Sour-dough biscuits with lots of fresh butter that she bought at the farmer's market. She had a large collection of recipes that she seldom used. She was her own chef," Natalia reflected.

"Now, she had a temper on a short fuse if anyone criticized her family. And, oh, she was a protestant, a member of the Evangelical Free Church. She was never a member of the Jewish faith. At times Julian would get her going by chiding her about being a protestant."

"They would jokingly argue: 'We just have the complete Bible,' she would say with a twinkle in her eye. 'You know I love you,' your father would reply, pulling her away from the stove and kissing her, 'even if you are a protestant,'" to which she would retort, 'And, I love you even if you are a Jew.' It was all in jest because Fannie loved your grandfather deeply."

Natalie would share highlights of the past every night until the list was exhausted. The children were as eager to hear what she had to say as the adults.

"You never got married Aunt Natalia?"

"No, I never met the right man. There was a Scottish gentleman named McDonald that I met at work. We dated for a while, but it never became a serious type of relationship. One day I came to work, and was informed by a fellow laborer that McDonald had quit and moved to Maryland. I never heard of him after that."

On Sundays Natalie attended church with the family, the first time she had ever been inside a Christian church. She watched intently as an adult couple was baptized. On the way home she asked, "What does it mean to be baptized?"

"A person is baptized when they become a believer in Jesus Christ and acknowledge their sins," said David. "It is like a soldier putting on his uniform. They are identifying as a Christian. Baptism symbolizes the death of Christ on the cross, his burial, and resurrection from the grave. It is a picture of the believer's death to sin and resurrection to new life in Christ. It also symbolizes the resurrection of the believer from the grave when Jesus comes back to the earth."

Natalie sat quietly contemplating his words. Finally, she said, "I want to be a Christian and be baptized." On the Sunday before she left to go back to New Orleans, with David standing beside her in the pool, she was baptized. Many in the congregation could not hold back the tears.

CHAPTER SEVEN

"**F**IVE DOLLARS, WHO will give me six for this nice walnut table?" shouted the auctioneer. The bidders hesitated hoping to buy the item cheap. Finally, a farmer lifted up two fingers. "Two I have, who will make it three? Three, and who will make it four? Four, I need four for this beautiful table. Some Shaker labored hours over this piece of furniture."

"Five," offered a lady in a print dress. The crowd suddenly came alive with anticipation, bids punctuating the air.

"Five, will anyone give six" urged the auctioneer, but no one did. In light of all there was to buy, the bidding on the table came to a close. "Five going once, five going twice, sold for five dollars!" said Colonel Everett Mahoney, the chief auctioneer. Mahoney was a man who could not speak in a normal conversation without stuttering, almost incoherently, but when he stood to auctioneer he spoke clearly as one of the fastest in the business. When he stood before the crowd, he gained his stride with a blast of words. That was the reason he waited to state the terms of sale. "Every item sold," he said with a slight stutter, "is final. No returns, no cancelation of bids, so look everything over before you bid. This exquisite furniture has been fashioned from the best black walnut, cherry, oak, ash, tulip and poplar. Do not hesitate to bid lest it get away from you!"

The crowd had already gathered in front of the Centre House when David and Henry sauntered across the unkempt yard. The once attractive living quarters, along with the other buildings, were now in stages of deterioration. Less than a handful of elderly Shakers did what they could to maintain the property. Glass windows were missing from their frames. Boards decayed in the structure of buildings. It was a different place from the Pleasant Hill they once knew and grew up in.

Adult and children's beds, cherry chests, tables and candle-stands, cast-iron stoves, spinning and flax wheels, woven rugs, corner cupboards, clocks, and other small items filled the large dining room. The auctioneer held up a glass handle kerosene lamp, purple with age, intact with a clean brass Imperial burner and chimney with a couple of bubbles in the glass. The lard-filled lamps had replaced the candles on the bedroom walls as early as 1848. By 1863, coal oil replaced lard in the lamps.

David was there to buy some items for his new antique shop. He bought many fine pieces, but he also purchased items that needed some repair. Some needed more attention than others. Items that other buyers let slip through their hands because of a slight imperfection like a scratch, a missing knob, a damaged top, a broken leg or a glass piece without a top.

On each repaired piece in his barn shop was a note that read, "Minor repair by a former Shaker." The note was of course referring to him. When asked if he knew this former Shaker he would shyly answer, "Quite well–you're looking at him." He often used this opportunity to share his testimony of how he came to Christ, having previously lived as a Shaker.

Behind the antique shop was a workroom where he repaired the damaged pieces. All the tools used were Shaker items he had bought at auctions, homemade calipers, claw hammers, wood mallets, horsehair brushes, drawing knives, saws, vice clamps, various types of wooden block planes, molding planes, hand drills, measuring tapes, and gauges all arranged neatly on the workshop walls.

His reputation as a collector and dealer in fine Shaker items grew as did his shop and repair reputation. Collectors from all over the nation, as well as some buyers from England, purchased items from him. Ruth, his nine-year-old daughter, occasionally traveled with him on buying trips, and became very knowledgeable about Shaker life and furniture. She once said to a perspective buyer, "He is very skilled repairman. Some of the finest families in town are his customers."

Myrtle Allen, a long-time collector and shop owner of Shaker items from Bardstown, Kentucky, died, and her entire collection, including her household Shaker furniture, was put up for auction. Unfortunately, a horrendous rainstorm began early in the morning of the auction and poured down until the late afternoon. Many buyers elected not to attend. David purchased three original wood stoves that heated the Shaker quarters, plates, eating utensils, wooden serving bowls, kitchen items, butter molds and churns, several large pieces of furniture, a blanket chest, a sugar chest, an oak sideboard, two maple washstands, six oak matching chairs, old glass stopper-bottles with Shaker labels, clothing, a round drop-leaf walnut table and five Shaker candle stands. He continued to purchase pieces privately from Sister Mary Settles, an elderly leader at Shaker Village, paying more than the items were worth at times because he knew the desperate situation the Shakers were in.

Henry shook his head as they loaded the items on the wagon, "I do not know who would be interested in knives, forks, spoons and these wood burning stoves."

"Some individuals are interested in anything Shaker," said David.

"Dad is right, Uncle Henry, I sold a stove last week after school."

The little shop grew into a larger barn filled with Shaker items. Letters from all over the county regularly filled the mailbox inquiring about different Shaker articles. Larger items were often shipped by train to distant destinations.

One of the last auctions they attended was at South Union Shaker Village in Logan County, Kentucky, some

200 miles away. They traveled over rugged back roads to get there. It took a full day to get there by horse drawn wagon and at least a long day to get back. David owned his own horse and wagon now and planned to make the trip alone.

The handbill announced the event as the "Last Call" to the Antique Auction on Saturday, April 8, held at the Railroad Station beginning at 10:30 A.M. There would be no reserves, open bidding only. The bill listed chest of drawers, tables both large and small, twin beds, wardrobes, cupboards, straight back chairs, and other articles too numerous to list– walnut, cherry and oak furniture dating back one hundred years.

Henry stopped by the bank, "Well, are we going to the auction Saturday at South Union?" he asked.

"I didn't know if you could be away from your practice for the trip. You know we are talking about a hard day's drive to South Union."

"Dr. Johnson has already agreed to see my patients. What time do we leave?"

"I don't think we can leave later than five o'clock in the morning. We will have to spend the night to be ready for the auction the next day. There is a board and breakfast about a mile from the Village. I have already secured a room. We will have to spend a second night after the auction packing up which will likely go into the late afternoon."

"It will be like old times," said Henry.

They arrived late at Jackson's bed and breakfast. After a good night's rest and breakfast the next morning they set out for South Union Shaker village. Like Pleasant Hill, the once beautiful buildings were in different stages of decay. Arriving early gave them an opportunity to examine all the items for defects and general condition. Other dealers were there early also. There were a lot of items that was going to require a fast auctioneer and workers to move the auction along.

"I doubt we are going to be able to get many deals here today," said David. "There are several high dollar dealers here that will be bidding for the good pieces, but there are several nice damaged pieces they probably won't want to fool with. I can repair any of them back to original."

The auction went as David predicted. Nice items without damage brought big bucks. Sure enough no one seemed to be interested in even slightly damaged items giving David opportunity to fill his wagon up with chairs of missing spindles, beds with broken foot boards, a large intricately carved oak side-board with a missing door, tables with damaged tops, a pair of old wooden works clocks that no longer worked due to broken cogs, a large cracked wooden bowl with a rolling pen, a cherry corner cupboard with two missing shelves and a knob on a drawer, various kitchen utensils, wooden wall lamp holders with broken or cracked knobs—all which could be returned to original condition at the hands of a skillful repairman. Of particular interest was a weathered sign announcing "Shaker Village of Logan County" that David bought.

The next morning before the sun came up the heavy-laden wagon pulled onto the road home to Nicholasville.

Dark rain clouds required a large tarp to shield the furniture from rain, and rain it did for about fifteen miles. Wearily, the pair pulled into the large barn doors, creaking as they opened on their well-worn hinges, around 10:30 p.m.

"The items will have to wait until Monday to unload. I am whooped," said David.

"Sounds good to me. My friend, you have a lot of repair work ahead of you."

"Yes, I know," said David closing the creaky doors. "I'll get the buggy out to take you home."

"No, it is only a few blocks away. I will be home before you can get hitched up. See you tomorrow," Henry bade, disappearing into the night.

It would be their last large auction they attended. Late at night, David worked on repairing and within a year everything was restored. He had hardly finished the last piece when he had a stroke on his left side, rendering him incapable of continuing repairing in the shop on Heathcliff Street. By this time, family members brought Shaker items to the shop before estates were put up for sale because they knew of David's fairness.

CHAPTER EIGHT

ONE OF THE last missionary-recruiting trips before the decline of Shaker Village was on November 9, 1868. Andrew Bloomberg arrived by boat in New York from a preaching trip in Sweden. On the warm evening of June 29, 1869, the *Orlando* pulled into port. Sweden was plagued by starvation, called "the year of great weakness" in the city of Satakunta and the surrounding regions. In three years, 270,000 people starved to death due to crop failure. The churches were exhausted of funds. There was little grain for bread and less grain for new crops. It was an awful time in the land and had been for several years.

With Bloomberg were eighteen Swedes that converted to the Shaker belief in order to immigrate to America and escape the threat of the starvation. Some later proved not be loyal to the Shaker belief in celibacy. Among them was

17-year-old Gavin Berglund, the only child of Ouintin and Ebba. His parents barely escaped a house fire on a cold December day while Gavin was away at school.

The *Orlando* pulled into the harbor, heading toward Castle Gardens where emigrants were processed before the Ellis Island Center was established. There was no Statue of Liberty to welcome them. The "lovely lady" was only a concept in the mind of the French sculptor Frederic Auguste Bartholdi. The torch-bearing arm was displayed at the Centennial Exposition in Philadelphia that year and later displayed at Madison Square Park in Manhattan for seven years due to lack of funding to complete the work. It would be ten years before the Lady would lift her arm in a dedication ceremony on Liberty Island greeting emigrants.

It was a rainy, windy day when Bloomberg pulled into Pleasant Hill on July 17, 1869 with his new converts from Sweden. Several Shakers laid down their tools of labor to greet them. From the different industries they came extending a right hand of fellowship to the new believers. The parents were assigned to the Centre Family and the children to the North Family House. At worship that evening they were introduced. Colin Berglund, who stood six foot four inches with blonde, curly hair, dark blue eyes, and a stocky build stood up when his name was called. He was handsome in every sense of the word with a pale complexion and a broad face.

When the meeting was dismissed David Matthews and Randall Blevins sauntered over to meet the youngest of the Swedes, all the others averaging in age from thirty to fifty. "Welcome to Pleasant Hill," greeted David, extending his hand. "This is Randall Blevins, my roommate."

"Thank you," said Gavin, in a heavy Swedish accent, "Gavin Berglund." His big smile revealed his fine set of healthy, white teeth. It was obvious that he was happy to meet some brethren near his own age.

David deliberated the fact that he would be leaving Shaker Village in a few weeks and that Randall would be leaving shortly thereafter. He would be working in the country store near the Shaker landing for his future father-in-law Thomas Miles and ultimately moving to Nicholasville to work at Town Square Bank. *When I leave the Village, Gavin would be a perfect hand on the Shaker Ferry. He is strong and pleasant. I must recommend him to Hillard for my replacement.*

Despite his innocent looks, Gavin was a troubled young man. One evening, after two other buildings had been set on fire and burned to the ground, the North Family barn was torched. Everything burned up in the fire: farm machinery, bags of wheat, hay, and straw; the cattle, sheep and goats barely escaped. Gavin had already come under suspicion because someone had seen him leave the barn at the time of the fire. A week later when questioned about his absence from the North quarters, he confessed to the crime. He was angry over being separated from his parents and relatives still in Sweden. The elders called a meeting to question him further and discovered he had set the other fires. Gavin was asked to leave Pleasant Hill, which he seemed glad to do seeing his attitude and strong desire to marry and have children.

The Shakers were glad to see him go, and he was glad to be asked to leave. He gathered his belonging together, an extra pair of shoes, two shirts, underwear, three pair of pants, an extra belt, and minimal toiletries into a suitcase, and walked to the Ferry on his way to Louisville. Three days later he was killed in a bar fight with a hotheaded Irishman that made fun of his clothes.

Violence was a regular occurrence on the Kentucky frontier in the nineteenth century. It was a time when men settled differences by duel, a fistfight, or vigilante action. Secret orders arose, some violent and others non-violent. Sometimes violence erupted to protect their secrets, at other times to make a statement.

Even the Freemasons, a secret group of hand-shakes, signs, code words and rituals, were not without stain. William Morgan, former Mason and newspaper editor, wrote a book entitled *Illustrations of Masonry*, exposing the Masonic ritual. When word got out about the book, Morgan began to suffer a series of mysterious experiences. He was arrested on bogus charges of failure to pay a debt and stealing a shirt and tie. There was an attempt to burn down his printing business. When his bond was paid on September 11, 1826 he mysteriously disappeared, never to be seen again. Ultimately, the local sheriff and three other men, all Masons, were arrested and sentenced to prison for their role in kidnapping Morgan and charged with his disappearance. This event ignited a powerful movement against Masonry, causing a number of lodges to shut down.

Another group arose among the Kentucky tobacco farmers. They were referred to by various names, but the one that was most prominent was the Night Riders. It was a militant group of tobacco farmers revolting against the American Tobacco Company, which held a monopoly and paid disastrously cheap prices to the tobacco farmers. The riders, dressed in hooded sheets to protect their identity, trampled crops, burn barns of tobacco, and destroyed tobacco warehouses to enforce compliance with the boycott against the American Tobacco Company.

Thomas Miles, David's father-in-law, not only owned the local grocery and hardware store, but grew three acres of tobacco on a farm he owned not far from his store. Early one morning, Billy, Sarah's little brother, knocked forcefully at David and Sarah's front door (though he is not so little anymore at age 27, weighing 202 pounds and standing at a height of six foot three inches tall). The sun was just beginning to peak over the horizon and the Matthews family had seated themselves at the breakfast table. In the middle of Luke's prayer, the impatient knock continued. David looked at Sarah and stood to see who was at the door.

With his hand raised to knock again, the door opened. "Bill, what are you doing out this early in the morning. Is there anything wrong?"

There was a desperation in his voice as Billy replied, "David, I need to talk to you privately."

Sensing the urgency of the matter, David escorted Billy to his office and motioned for Billy to have a seat.

"Dad has heard that the Night Riders are planning on burning down his barn and tobacco crop tonight. He is planning on securing himself with his shotgun inside the barn. He told me that if anyone walks through those barn doors with a torch in his hand, he was going to blow them away."

David ran his hands through his long, black hair, "You know it has been rumored that your grandfather on your mother's side is a member of the Night Riders."

"Yes, I know. Dad told me himself. David you have to talk to Dad. He will listen to you."

"Certainly your Dad has a right to defend his property against vandals, and he has a right to sell his tobacco to whoever and whatever he wishes. He can't be in that barn alone. As soon as the bank closes, I will be there."

Thomas Miles stepped outside his front door as David pulled up. "Why David, what are you doing here?"

Wrapping his horse's reigns around a small locust tree he said, "I heard you might have trouble tonight, and I came over to be with you."

Turning around as Billy came out the door, "You were not supposed to tell anyone. David can't be mixed up in this."

Retrieving his hunting gun from his holster on the saddle he retorted, "We are family, and you are not going to face these hoodlums alone."

"You are just in time for supper. Frances has your favorite: boiled cabbage, county ham, potatoes and corn."

"Sounds good to me!"

"David, what are you doing here?" Francis threw her arms around him and drew him close. "I guess I know the answer to that question. I'm really not surprised to see you here."

Thomas offered the prayer thanking God for providing food in such a needy world and asked that He protect those gathered around the table from any harm. A chorus of amens filled the room.

Just before dark Thomas, David, and Billy entered the barn; each had a shotgun. Stacked bales of hay formed a protective barrier against gunfire. They waited, talking softly in order not to alert the Night Riders. Thomas pulled out his pocket watch that read twelve o'clock. "I think they must have decided against coming or we got a wrong tip." He was just about ready to call it a night when they heard horses coming up to the barn. They grew tense as they waited. It sounded like around twenty horses outside. Men talking in low voices approached the barn doors. Three of them lit kerosene-soaked torches as they moved closer to the door. Thomas pulled the harmers back on both barrels. So did David and Billy. They waited for the barn door to open. It was a tense moment. They had arranged the bales of hay so that their guns would fit down beside them giving just enough room to see any activity at the door. Thomas had told his sons not to fire unless a torch was thrown in the barn.

Outside, it sounded like an argument between the men. Suddenly, it grew deathly quiet. The men waited anxiously. One torch after another was extinguished.

Footsteps were heard leading away from the barn. Then the sound of horse's hoofs disappeared into the night.

Thomas lifted his hand signaling not to move. "It might be a ploy to get us to show ourselves," he said in a whisper. After about fifteen minutes the men eased the hammers back on their guns and walked quietly to the front of the barn. The Night Riders had left. For what reason they had no idea. The next night they waited again, but nothing happened. The Night Riders never came back.

"The Lord answered our prayers for safety," said David, "and delivered us from the hand of trouble."

"Yes, He certainly did," said Thomas, his arms around his son's shoulders as they walked back to the house.

CHAPTER NINE

IT WAS SIX-THIRTY in the morning. The soft light of the large kerosene lamp hanging from the ceiling of his Dad's study drifted into the hallway next to Luke's bedroom. On the brass-colored front was the company's name Lomax and a patent-date of September 22, 1879. Dangling below a shiny, brass smoke-bell was a prism ring hung with 38 long, glass prisms. Large painted roses adorned the shade. It had been a gift from David's long-time friend, Dr. Henry DeVoe. Henry and his father-in-law Dr. Oscar Thompson had purchased an old drug store that had been closed for several years in nearby Wilmore, Ky. The hanging lamp was retrieved from a dusty backroom. It was missing the top shade, but the bottom part of the lamp was intact. Henry knew David and Sarah liked antique items and was delighted to share it with them. Sarah employed a local artist to paint a new shade for the lamp. The shade matched the rose covered design perfectly.

David got up around six in the morning to stoke the fireplace that had burned low during the night. The bright embers soon quickly set the ash logs ablaze. When Luke, now nine years old, crawled out of bed, the heat was already penetrating the hallway. He pulled the quilt that grandmother Miles had given up around his neck. Benjamin squirmed, turned over, snuggling up to his own cover.

Luke knew his Dad would be in his study reading his Bible and praying before the day began. His Bible was in his lap, and he had fallen asleep across some notes he was making on the Book of Daniel for a talk he was asked to give in the coming Sunday evening service. His pastor Bill Barnes was preaching during a revival at Valley View, Ky. The men of the church were filling the pulpit. His pen was still in his hand beside his head on the desk. Luke gently nudged his Dad's shoulder waking him. David lifted his head surprised at Luke's presence.

"What are you doing up so early son?" inquired David, wiping the sleep from his eyes.

"I did not sleep well last night. I had terrible dreams through the night."

"What kind of dreams Luke?"

"I dreamed I was standing before a runaway horse. There was a lady and a little boy in the carriage. The lady was screaming for me to get out of the way."

"I am not sure that the dream has meaning," pondered David.

"I have had that dream three times before."

"It must have some significance then."

"Dad, Brother Barnes preached on the Prodigal Son a few weeks back. He titled his sermon, 'How Lost Is Lost?', and I have been thinking about that sermon ever since."

David drew Luke into his arms as hot tears streamed from his eyes onto his nightgown. Neither spoke for a few moments.

"I figured out that I am lost. I believe in Jesus, but I have never accepted him as my Savior."

"Is that what you want to do Luke? You do not have to wait until Brother Barnes gives an invitation during a church service to accept Jesus."

"Yes, Dad, I want that more than anything." David explained how he had received Christ as a young man with the help of his roommate Randall Blevins. Luke bowed his head and asked Jesus to forgive his sins and come live in his heart.

"Were you baptized when you were growing up at Pleasant Hill?"

"No, the Shakers didn't baptize their converts. Besides I never signed the covenant, so actually I never was a true Shaker. They believed that the baptism of Jesus was not a baptism of water, but of the Holy Spirit. That is, they didn't believe that baptism by water was an ordinance of the church. When the Holy Spirit came down at Jesus's baptism by John the Baptist they considered it a figure, and the importance of the event was not immersion under the water but the anointing of the Holy Spirit symbolized by the dove coming down on Jesus."

"In fact, they didn't observe the Lord's Supper as an ordinance of the church either. It is complicated to explain, but they believed that Jesus came back as Ann Lee, the founder of the Shakers in America. They did not believe that Jesus was the physical Son of God but the spiritual Son. They also believed that Ann Lee was a spiritual daughter of God. They believed that just as Jesus became the Christ so did Ann Lee. Of course, there is no biblical basis for such ideas. In the early church, the first century church, believers were immersed in water and observed the Lord's Supper as a symbol of His coming back to earth. Ann Lee claimed that Jesus came to her and revealed to her that she was His second coming. This is heresy, of course."

"That is very interesting Dad. Why are you weeping?"

"Because what you have done makes me so happy."

Sarah had been standing in the doorway listening. Her eyes were wet as she reached out to hug her son.

"Well, I didn't know it would make you two so happy or I would have done it sooner."

They hugged and laughed before Luke returned to his room. Luke was whistling "I am Bound for the Promised Land" when Sarah entered the kitchen to fix breakfast, "You must hurry boys. It will be time to leave for school soon."

Luke returned to his room to wake Benjamin, who squirmed and resisted the nudge to his shoulder but eventually surrendered to the aroma of eggs and bacon wafting into the room. He rose up, wiped his eyes, and smiled a "good morning."

"Benjamin, I just asked Jesus to save me," his parents heard him say, "I can't wait to tell my friends at school today."

"I did that last year in Bible school. Welcome, brother, into the family of God."

"Why didn't you tell us?"

"I was waiting for you."

Sarah smiled as she placed the silverware around the table.

"We can be baptized together. Sunday we will tell Brother Barnes."

"Suits me!"

Breakfast was interesting that morning. As they held hands around the table, David asked Sarah to lead the prayer. "For this food, Father, we are very grateful in such a hungry world. Lord, we are so thankful for our children. Thank you for sending Jesus to die for our sins. Thank you that Benjamin and Luke have accepted you as Savior. Send your angels today to watch over and protect them. Amen!"

The prayer prompted Luke's curiosity. "Dad, do you think we have a personal angel that watches over us?"

Benjamin jumped into the conversation. "I believe we do."

"You seem so certain, son. Have you ever seen an angel?" asked his mother.

"Well, I have seen what my angel can do. Last week, I was walking to school, the day Luke was home with a sore throat, past the Wilder home when his pit bulls, one is white and brown and the other is black and chocolate, began to growl. Clearance Jordon, a friend at school, told me that Mr. Wilder trained them to fight other dogs."

"So, what happened?" asked Luke, leaning in closer.

"They weren't chained and jumped the fence. They came after me, growling fiercely. I just stood there. I knew I couldn't outrun them. Then, I asked Jesus if he wasn't busy to send one of His Angels to protect me. The dogs stopped in their tracks, turned, and began to whine like someone was about to hurt them. They had the weirdest look on their faces as they ran back and jump the fence into their yard. When I pass now, they do not even bark. I think Jesus sent one of his angels to protect me."

Sarah looked at David and back to Benjamin, "You need to take a different route to school from now on."

"I am going to have a talk with Mr. Wilder," said David. "You could have really been hurt by those dogs. As for the angels, Jesus says in Matthew 18:10 that the angels watch over children. It isn't clear if each believer has an angel or if the Lord sends angels on occasions when we need help."

"The nation of Israel has an archangel named Michael," added Sarah. "It says so in Daniel 10:2, and he protects them."

"There are many references in the Bible relating to angels. An angel delivered Peter from prison in Acts 12. We know they rescue God's children from danger, give guidance, and encourage." David pushed away from the table, "You guys are going to be late for school unless you hurry. Brush your teeth and off with you. Also, do not go by the Wilder house."

Standing, "I know there are shadows that pass my bedroom window at times. It is not a large shadow, just a small, quick shadow. No one looks in and I am not afraid. I just assumed it was my angel passing by," commented Luke.

"We can continue this discussion tonight," replied Sarah.

At the evening devotions Benjamin sat next to his dad, huddled up close. David read from 2 Kings 6:14-17: "The king of Syria dispatched his army to Dothan to capture Elisha. His servant came rushing in exclaiming that the hillsides were filled with fully armed Syrian soldiers. Elisha sent the young man back out to look closer as he prayed that God would open to his eyes to their protection. A greater army of angels in chariots of fire stood ready to defend the prophet and his servant."

Benjamin's blue eyes were big and bright, as he comprehended the greatness of God. Luke registered no surprise, whispering, "I hope I can see my angel one of these days."

Benjamin closed with prayer as they held hands before the fireplace. "Dear Jesus, thank you for protecting me the other day with your angel. Protect Luke, Ruth, Mom and Dad through the day and in the nights ahead. I love you Jesus. Amen!"

Three days later David would experience his own angel as two robbers entered the bank where he worked. Marion Noland, the bank president, was out of town and John Martin, his assistant, was on vacation. David was at the cashier's counter counting the receipts as Bret Williams and Regina Paxton were preparing to close the vault.

A tall, burley man stepped through the front door as he pulled up a handkerchief around his face. Stringy grey hair hung down from a grey, faded John Bull top hat. He pulled a small, silver, breech-loading Derringer pistol from his waistcoat. There was a missing top button from the tarnished brass buttons running down his wrinkled waistcoat.

The second robber appeared, a gangly, much younger male following close behind the first man. He pulled a blue handkerchief up in one quick move, covering his own face. He seemed extremely nervous at the front door, pulling the blinds down indicating the bank was closed. He had the appearance of an immigrant freshly from Castle Gardens in New York wearing what looked like a flat, worn leather railroad engineer's cap. He had long black hair. A short brown coat covered a heavy pleated yellow shirt that looked as though he had slept in it the night before. His pants were baggy, wrinkled farm pants. He kept looking at his partner and then back out the shade.

"Get your hands up! This is a robbery," growled the older man, now standing before the single open cashier's counter where David stood calmly. Bret and Regina heard the command from the back room.

David silently prayed, "Lord, today if you have an angel to spare, I need his help." He observed that the man had a single-shot weapon, while the man at door appeared unarmed.

Bret lifted his finger to his lips indicting silence to Regina as he picked up a cashier's tray and entered whistling as if he knew nothing was happening. David seemed as surprised as the robbers when he sauntered in from the back. He wasn't sure if he were signaling his presence so as not to get shot or to throw the robbers off. The man still had the gun leveled at David behind the cage.

His memory was flooded with an incident that took place a few years back when was working on the Shaker Ferry. The gunman had a large, memorable scar on his forehead, stood within eight feet of David, his pistol pointed directly at him, the cylinder turned slowly aligning the bullet in the chamber, the hammer cocked, he was beginning to squeeze the trigger when he was commanded to hold his fire by the leader of the group. That day he was scared stiff. He could not move and was hardly able to speak. Today, he had a calmness that mystified even him. Perhaps, it was his angel calming his nerves.

He winked at Bret as he took the tray from his hands and moved from behind the cage. "What are you doing," asked the robber. "Stand still."

David kept moving out and toward the man. "I can hardly hand over the money unless I bring it to you."

"Ugh! I guess you are right."

David was now standing face to face with the robber less than three feet away. As the man lowered his pistol to take the tray David suddenly flipped the money tray upward, knocking the gun from his hand to the floor. Surprised, the man let out a loud profanity as he lunged toward David. Bret was stunned. The two men wrestled on the floor as the second robber rushed out the door to his horse tied at the rail. By this time, Bret had reached David's side to help subdue the robber. His mask had slipped under his chin revealing his identity as a recent escapee from the Nicholasville jail, arrested for drunken and disorderly conduct on Friday night. David remembered him from the church service held Sunday at the local jail by his pastor and visitors from the church, including him.

Unknown by all, Regina had quietly slipped out the back door for the Sherriff's Office two blocks away. He was entering the door when he saw David wrestling the robber to the floor. He and his Deputy rushed over to restrain the robber, cuff him, and take him to jail.

"I didn't know you had it in you David," commended Bret. "I was puzzled as to what to do. I would have given him the money."

"It was nothing my Angel couldn't handle," he beamed.

"You will both be called as witnesses," explained the Sherriff. "It is pretty much a closed case since we have the culprit."

"There was a second robber, I think a young man," replied David.

"Oh, we have him too. Caught him running from the bank to his horse."

CHAPTER TEN

BY 1870, RUMORS of problems at Pleasant Hill began to surface; young people were departing the faith. The Society was failing to find new leadership to take the place of the aging leaders that were now dying off like flies. Internally, there were financial commitments largely due to the careless dealings of James Dunlavy. Dunlavy soared up through the ranks of leadership after replacing Rufus Bryant, a paralytic through a fall from the steps leading up to the back of his house some years back. After Dunlavy's death on August 17, 1886, his disastrous financial blunders were discovered–commitments made without the permission of the other church leaders.

He had invested Society monies in two hundred and fifty shares of Nevada gold mining stock, which turned out to be valueless. There were others that proved to be an albatross around the neck of the fledging few members of the Society.

The railroad that the Shakers welcomed in the beginning became a problem for marketing their own goods. Large companies could transport their products at a cheaper price.

Internally, there was conflict with the leadership of the Pennebaker brothers; William trained as a doctor and Francis as a dentist. In their training they were introduced to the more progressive world, which they tried to initiate into Shaker life.

Financial disaster with the loss of the North cow barn affected their now struggling community. Later, the Centre Family's large barn, shops, and outbuildings were also burned to the ground by an arsonist of their own community.

An often overlooked contributing factor to the Shaker's decline was the establishment of denominational orphanages in Kentucky by the Presbyterians, Baptist, and Methodist. The Baptist established what became Spring Meadows Children's Home near Louisville on June 30[th,] 1869. In 1871, the Methodist began the Widows and Orphans Home in Louisville, a home for orphaned children of the Civil War. They later located with fifty-six children and a small staff to a farm in Versailles, Kentucky. Later, in 1904, the Presbyterians began an orphanage in a house in Bowling Green with money left by one of its previous members for the sole purpose of accommodating orphans.

Orphans from distant cities were brought to Pleasant Hill in the beginning. This was limited with the church orphanages popping up across America, as well as non-denominational groups.

Newly passed Kentucky laws made it harder to adopt children that had become the life's blood for Shaker growth. This meant that the Society had to be more diligent in obeying the laws of the land concerning adoption lest they be charged with kidnapping. The well for growth began to dry up.

The first two years of the Civil War saw hoards of military companies stopping over to be fed by the Shakers, depleting their basements of stored foods. It became necessary to hold a meeting to discuss their desperate situation of food shortage. They were greatly relieved when, at the end of the first two years of the Civil War, large armies stopped coming.

Disease reduced their numbers. In 1813, around sixty people died of the cold plague alone. Other diseases such as whooping cough, influenza, measles and mumps, in addition to several unidentifiable ailments including fevers and chills, took their toll on the Shakers.

David and Henry decided to visit the Village, hoping for a warm reception, and they got it. They were greeted as old friends. Afterward, tea and delicious cookies served by their former teacher Mary Settles. She talked about the old times, asked them about their families, the type of work they were doing, and the future of Pleasant Hill. When she spoke of the decline of the buildings, the few Shakers still left, made up mostly the very young and the very old, she looked away wistfully as she talked of the great leaders of the past and Mother Ann Lee: "It was all a beautiful reality at one time, fields of grain, cattle grazing, the industries busy producing their wares, but all that is past now. The West Lot family dropped to less than eleven members and had to be disbanded. The shops of the Village are all in decay, and there is no one left to perform the crafts. Almost no one is left to promote Shaker beliefs."

When they realized she was tiring, David asked if they could see their old room in the East House Family building, before they returned home. "Certainly," replied Sister Settles, "I will get you the key. All the building lacked maintenance due to dwindling funds. Shingles were blown from roofs by summer storms; windows were broken in vacant buildings; once painted family homes were shabby looking, the paint peeling from their structures. After 1885, the Shakers no longer danced in their meetings, which had become the centerpiece of their worship services. Curtains hung in the Centre Family dwelling over the previously uncovered windows, some of the women no longer wore the traditional Shaker bonnets, mirrors and pictures hung on the once bare walls, a practice previously considered worldly by the Shakers. The former prosperous garden seed industry had closed its doors. The broom factory where six workers produced 50,000 brooms in one year, providing desperately needed income for the Village, had closed its operation years ago. An iron bar across the front door with a large brass lock protected it from vandalism.

"Doesn't look like what it did when we left," observed Henry as they walked along the once immaculate main road from the Centre Family building to the now vacant East House where they had lived during their tenure there. Grass grew up in patches, weeds were waist deep, and seedling trees dotted the landscape.

"No, I was just noticing that. It is sad in many ways. Not many children playing on the lawns. No busy wagons bearing their goods to market. And did you notice how few cattle are in the fields? The Shakers have fallen on hard times."

They nudged the yellow, faded door open, creaking on its rusty hinges, climbing the long flight of stairs, on the left side, the male side, as they had done so many times before as boys. It was the first family dwelling built by the Shakers at Pleasant Hill—a three-story construction that included a huge attic with living quarters on the second floor, the women on one side and the men on the other, with a spacious basement. Set on a limestone foundation, the lumber materials were all taken from the forests around Pleasant Hill. Built by Shaker hands, it took six years to complete. Construction was under the direction of Micajah Burnett. It was empty now with dust collecting on the furniture and most everything in its original place.

At the top of the steps David stopped abruptly. The door to their old room stood open. Henry bumped into him. "What is it?"

"I guess I just wasn't ready to revisit our past."

"But it is just an old room."

"No, it isn't just any old room, it is our room. It is where we lived growing up here at Pleasant Hill." The room had two simple beds, straw mattresses, covered by the same patch quilts, with the bag of spices tied at the end to ward off insects, including bed bugs. No one really knew if it worked or not. Like all other home remedies, the Shakers boasted to cure ills. They silently stood there at the ends of the single beds. It was a simple room with two thatched chairs, a stove, a walnut chest of draws for each resident, pegs on the walls for coats and hats, and a single lamp stand on the east wall. It was all there as they left it, or those who followed.

David stood there in dead silence reliving the long conversations about the Civil War, the death of Lincoln, the strange beliefs of the Shakers, about Sarah, and the dangerous night visits to the Shaker Landing.

"What are you thinking?" asked Henry.

"Just about old times when we lived here, Brother Andrew bringing us to our room for the first time, the long conversation that first night that brought him back to our doorway warning us that it was past bedtime, descending the creaky steps back to his apartment at the foot of the stairs. I was thinking of the long boat ride from the orphanage in New Orleans to here, Elder Micajah describing to us thirteen boys what Pleasant Hill was like. I can still see the eagerness in the older boy's eyes and the uncertainty some of the rest of us felt." Changing the subject, "I am going to ask Sister Mary if they will sell the furniture in this room to us."

Surprised, Henry said, "You can have it all. Nothing for me to remember from the past but the pain of living here, leaving, and the war."

"Are you sure?'

"I am certain."

"All right, I am going for it."

As they turned to leave, David lingered and smiled. They were promptly back at the Centre House, knocking on the door. Sister Mary Settles opened it.

"Sister Mary, I was wondering if you ever considered selling the items out of our old room."

"What items in particular were you interested in?"

"Well," David fumbled for words, "all of it in our old room on the second floor of the East Family building. It was the front corner room."

"Actually, we are planning on selling some of the furniture at a future auction. I cannot see why we couldn't let you have it. I would like to give it to you," she hesitated, "but we are in desperate times. What do you think everything is worth?"

"I was hoping you would have a figure in mind."

"Since, you lived in that room, do you think $15.00 is too much?"

"I will give you $25.00 for it." In future purchases, he always gave her more than she asked for items.

"When can you come and get it?"

"I will bring a wagon for it next Tuesday, around ten thirty, if that suits you?"

"Tuesday it is!" She extended her hand to shake on it, sealing the deal.

David could hardly contain himself as they returned to the buggy and headed to Nicholasville. Mary Settles stood at the door waving as they left. Tears filled her eyes, not over selling the furniture, but by the visit of the two young men.

Tuesday at 10:29 a.m. David and Henry pulled onto the Ferry. Hillard was still captain but much older. He had aged as all of them had. His hair was almost white. Two young men stood at the far end, both no more than fifteen years old, that maneuvered the ropes to cross the river. Hillard hugged them as tears flooded his eyes. This was not the first time he had seen them since they left the Village. "We missed you coming over last week. Someone said you were in Harrodsburg."

"Yes, I had to buy some supplies. Ben Stevens is my main helper on the Ferry now. I am one of the few remaining younger Elders, and I'm sixty-three; so, it falls to me to do the distant shopping."

They pulled off the Ferry as tears streamed down Hillard's face. "Come back before seven o'clock so we can talk some more before we close down." Up the hill, around the curve, to the Village they traveled. In less than fifteen minutes they pulled up before the Center House where Sister Mary Settles was waiting in a rocking chair on the front porch. She stood as they pulled up. Two young Shakers around twelve years old were waiting with her to help load the furniture.

David handed her an envelope. "I wish it could be more, but it is the twenty dollars we agreed on."

After dismantling the beds, they helped load the items on the wagon. Wrapping the lamp in newspaper and removing the clothes from the large walnut chiffonier, they watched as David held a pair of pants up measuring them against his waist. "I believe these are a pair of my old pants."

"But they won't fit now," teased Henry.

"No, but they might fit Luke. Anyway, I am going to keep them."

Henry searched through the few remaining clothes, observing, "Nothing of mine in here."

"No, after you left your clothes were given to a boy that had just come to the North Family; I forget his name."

Henry heard a moan of one of the young men helping to load the items. He noticed a couple of drops of blood on the floor oozing from his tattered shoe.

"What is wrong with your foot? Sit down here and let me take look at it."

"It is alright," said the boy.

"No, it's not. It is bleeding." The young boy named Tom sat down in one of the chairs and stuck his foot out for examination. His shoes were terribly tattered, worn out long ago.

Henry removed the shoe carefully revealing his blistered and bleeding foot. "You need a new pair of shoes. Let me look at the other foot. It was the same. The blood inside the shoe stuck to the leather. "I want you to soak your feet tonight in warm water. Tomorrow, I will bring you a new pair of shoes and some ointment to heal your feet up. Why hasn't Dr. Pennebaker tended your feet?"

"Dr. Pennebaker doesn't come to the Village as a doctor anymore. There was some kind of dispute among him, Elder Dunlavy, and the leadership over some changes to the Shaker beliefs. It was reported that while Dr. Pennebaker was in medical school he became more progressive in his philosophy of Shaker beliefs, encouraging more openness in an attitude toward other denominations and encouraged more individual enterprises. It was further inflamed when Pennebaker led the West Family to cease support of the Society. It all came to a climax when he set aside over six hundred acres of land for himself and his brother. It was then that he stopped coming to the Village to attend the medical needs of those of us that were left."

"I will take care of that. I am a certified doctor in Nicholasville and each Saturday I will be here to meet the medical needs of the Society. My nurse will accompany me for the needs of the female residents," Henry stated decidedly.

"You would do that?" asked William, the other young boy, standing in the doorway.

"Of course I will do it, and it won't cost anyone a penny. I will be back tomorrow with ointment and medicines. Pass the word around to the others. I will be back each week around two-thirty. I see patients in Nicholasville until twelve o'clock. David and I grew up in Shaker Village. This was our room before we left. I left to join the Union Army. David left to get married. Tom, you continue to rest and we will load the wagon. Then we will give you both a ride back to the Centre Family quarters."

The last piece of furniture loaded was the chair that Tom was sitting in. There was now a small puddle of blood on the floor. William helped him hobble down the stairs to the back of the wagon.

After dropping the boys off at the Center Family House, there was a long silence as they drove back down the road to the Ferry. "That was a great pledge you made to those boys."

"It is the least I can do. The Shakers fed and clothed me for several years."

"I want to come back and be your assistant."

"You are always welcome," said Henry. "I will pick you up at your house a little before two. The bank closes at twelve, right?"

David and Henry sang Christian hymns on their way back to Nicholasville after a short stopover with Hillard at the Ferry. They talked about their visit with Sister Mary Settles and how warm she was toward them. "Yes, most of the Shakers have mellowed in their beliefs."

This was the beginning of a renewed relationship with the Shakers. They took shoes and used clothing regularly to the Village, the Shakers having modified their clothing restrictions. Now, the youth as well as some adults looked like their contemporaries. In fact, the women and men, while always dressing virtuously, wore more modern clothes but always down to the ankles. Dress was hard to govern with families joining the Shakers for financial or material reasons as the believers entered the latter part of the 19th century. Previously, most of the clothing was made by the believers themselves–women for women's apparel and tailors for the men. Some of the elderly adults retained the old styles until their death. The girls wore white caps and the men wore hats.

After some chitchat for a brief time with Hillard, they said their farewells and headed back to Nicholasville, back to the normal way of life—Henry to his practice of medicine and David to the bank.

CHAPTER ELEVEN

IT WAS EARLY in the morning on a beautiful October day. The leaves had already turned various colors. David was working on a loan for a new couple to the city. Sarah, an early arriver, had already gone to school and was preparing for the day's assignments. Their children were growing up. Luke was eleven and in the tenth grade. Ruth, in the seventh grade, had walked to school with her mother. Luke lagged behind to walk with his friend Johnny Roberts.

David looked up from his work after hearing a loud commotion down the street. He thought little of it, continuing to work the figures when someone knocked loudly at the front door, shouting something about "Luke is hurt in the street." He jumped up and ran to the door turning the large brass key in the lock as quickly as possible.

It was Tom Marshall, a lawyer three doors down from the bank. "David, you must come quickly. Luke has been run over by a runaway horse. I did not get all the details, but he looks like he is badly hurt." Locking the front door, he ran to the crowd gathered on the Main Street. Luke was bleeding from his mouth. His eyes rolled back in his head as he uttered "Dad" before going unconscious.

Mary Willis ran up to David screaming something about her run-away horse and Luke running into the street to stop it. David hardly heard her story as he leaned down and scooped Luke up in his arms. "Will someone take us to Dr. Henry DeVoe's office?"

"Yes, my carriage is right here. I saw it all. Get in," said Ben Stokes, the town's Mayor.

Running up to the buggy was Mary Willis, sobbing "I am so sorry. There was nothing I could do."

"It is all right Mary; you can tell me later what happened. Right now, I need to get Luke to the doctor."

Ben Stokes helped lift Luke into the back of the carriage as David held him in his arms. Blood was oozing from his mouth and ears. "Hurry Ben. Luke is really hurt," cried David. Ben cracked the whip over his horse as they spend down the road to Elm Street.

Having heard the news, Henry was holding the door for them and helped lift Luke onto the examining table. His nurse Millie Brown was heating water to remove the blood. Luke ceased to groan as he lay on the table. Henry didn't ask David to wait outside as he bent over Luke examining his eyes. There was a large knot on his head. After a few moments Henry turned to David. "We must get him to the Lexington Hospital."

"We can all go in my buggy," offered Ben Stokes.

"Mille, take care of things until I return."

"Certainly, doctor."

"We cannot wait for Sarah to get here. Luke is seriously injured, and I am not sure he can make it alive to the hospital, but we must go now."

David was pale as he acknowledged that Henry was correct. He obediently lifted his son into the waiting buggy. Luke groaned as they turned onto the main road to the Lexington Hospital. "Hold on Luke, we are getting help for you," whispered David, as a large tear dropped onto Luke's face. He tried to hold back the tears, but it was too much for him to bear. His son was possibly dying in his arms.

On the way, Ben told David what happened. Luke was walking to school with a friend when the horse of Mary Willis got spooked by a barking dog that kept biting at the horses' heals. Mary tried to calm her horse down as he bolted down the street. Luke was walking on the left side of the street when he saw what was happening. Instinctively he ran into the street to stop the horse. The horse never slowed as he ran over Luke. I know the back wheel ran over Luke's head. David, your son is a hero."

The Emergency Staff rushed Luke down the hall to the surgery room. David and Ben waited outside. Henry followed the gurney in. Sarah arrived a few minutes later along with a young couple from the church. She was sobbing as she ran to David. "What in the world happened?"

"There was a run-away horse pulling a buggy with Mary Willis and her little boy in it. Luke ran out and tried to stop it. The horse ran over him."

"What does the doctor say?"

"Henry said it looks very bad." She began to sob harder throwing her head on David's shoulder. "Whatever will we do if..." The doctor came from the surgery room, removing his mask as he entered. Blood soaked his uniform.

"I am very sorry to tell you that your son died of a hemorrhage of the brain. We did all we could. I am sorry," said the chief surgeon. Henry followed him through the door, his eyes drenched in tears. He threw his arms around David and Sarah and wept with them.

The funeral held two days later was the largest the town had ever seen. School was dismissed. Kids from Luke's class lined up before the casket. Staff from the bank and almost every business in town came to offer their condolences. Some were people David and Sarah had never met–people from country-farmers, herders, and tenant workers. The line went on and on at the viewing. Finally, at 12:30 p.m. the front doors were closed, and the last couple came down the aisle. John Martin, Vice President of the bank, with his wife, and eleven-year-old daughter began crying before they reached the casket. They stood there silently for a while, and then turned to the family. John could not speak for weeping nor could his wife.

Their daughter Evelyn took Sarah's hand and said, "I was in Luke's class. He sat behind me. He was a very nice boy. I am sorry for what has happened. It was so much like him to think of others. I remember a thin, poor boy named Billy that was bullied by an older boy, and Luke challenged him to stop badgering the boy. The bully just walked away, and Luke put his arm around Billy and said, 'Will you be my friend? There is an empty seat behind me. I will ask our teacher if you can sit there.' Then Billy replied, gratefully 'I would like that.' He was never picked on after that." After her story, she added, "He was a great witness for Christ as his Savior. One morning he came to school telling everyone in the class how he was saved the night before."

Sarah gave way to her emotions at the grave, throwing herself upon the casket, uttering, "O God, why did you let this happen?" David put his arm around her and wept as he patted the face of Luke. It took a long time for her to get past blaming God for the accident.

"We live in a fallen world and bad things happen to good and bad people," said the Pastor in a sermon. "Mankind in the Garden made the choice to sin. It wasn't God's will that they disobey Him. God's only Son paid the price for our sins. One day Jesus is coming back to take us home with Him and we will see our loved ones there." Sarah was never the same after that sermon. On his tombstone were the words, "Luke Matthews, son of David and Sarah Matthews–a child of the King."

Night after night Sarah would rise from their bed and go into the family room where she could be heard weeping and praying, "O help me Lord to understand Luke's death. Help me to know your presence and peace." David, awakened, would go to her and put his arms around her. One night Sarah crawled back into the bed and fell to asleep immediately. The next morning the household was awakened by singing from the kitchen. "You are cherry this morning," David remarked as he bent over to kiss her.

"I have something wonderful to tell you. It happened last night as I was struggling to pray."

"What happened?" David asked as Ruth entered the room, wiping the sleep from her eyes. "What happened Mother?" Benjamin slipped through the doorway and took a seat at the table waiting for breakfast.

"Last night, as I was asking the Lord to reveal to me why He allowed Luke's death, a figure surrounded by a bright light appeared and said, 'I am taking care of Luke until you get here.' Just as quickly as He appeared, He vanished. That was all He said. I know it was Jesus and I no longer have to know why because I know the Lord is taking care of Luke."

"That is wonderful dear. God comes to us in the sunshine as well as in our dark experiences," he said, pulling her close.

Benjamin, two years younger than Luke, began to sleep in Luke's bed, the bed that had belonged to David at Shaker Village. When Benjamin was twelve, his father told him about his experiences as a Shaker boy at Pleasant Hill. His bright eyes sparkled as he listened. Sarah and David sat in the flower garden behind their house. "You can't protect him against harm," David whispered as an aside to Sarah, "You must let him grow up like other boys, playing sports, and skinning his knees when he falls."

"I know you are right," she said softly as she put her arm through his and smiled. "It is just…"

David finished her sentence "It is just that you want to protect him, so that something doesn't happen like what happened to Luke. You can't protect him forever. Let him grow up and be a regular boy."

The doorbell rang. It was Henry and Elizabeth with their two children. They had been invited for dinner. Sarah cooked a pot roast with onions, potatoes, and carrots. Elizabeth brought hot butter rolls. "It was delicious, as usual," said Henry as he pushed back from the table. "Yes, indeed it was," agreed Elizabeth. "I particularly like the brown gravy that you make to go with it and the cranberry salad with walnuts."

While the children played board games in the living room, their parents played rook at the kitchen table. David and Henry played against their able wives that usually won. "Tonight, we are going to beat you," chided David.

"Well, I bid 100," teased Sarah, "and no kicking under the table."

"Now, you know we wouldn't do that," said Henry, laughing.

"Only, if you have a winning hand," retorted Elizabeth.

It was Friday night and the couples played until eleven o'clock, the women winning again. "Now, who did you say was going to win tonight?"

"Henry, I think we are going to have to find a new game. Rook doesn't seem to be our suit."

"Have you heard from Randall lately?" asked Henry.

"I received a letter from him about a scandal he covered involving the city mayor that led to the Mayor being charged in a corruption scam. Randall and his family were threatened several times. He feared they would bomb his home. Emily was accosted in the grocery store by a stranger threating her life and the life of their children. They had to be taken to school under police supervision. The local bomb squad was called in to investigate a suspicious package on their front porch. There was no return address and the box contained a note that simply gave a date for what they did not know. It went on until the Mayor, you know Emily's father had been Mayor previously, was tried and sentenced for channeling funds into a special secret account. The police escorted Randall to his job as Editor of the Cleveland Ohio Sentinel even after they indicted the Mayor. They plan to come down August 27-30. You and Elizabeth must plan to come over for dinner while they are here."

CHAPTER TWELVE

JOHN MARTIN WAS appointed president of the bank after Stephen Noland died of a massive heart attack. Shortly after, the Trustees elected David as Vice-President, following John's recommendation. It came with a hefty raise, also recommended by John.

Nicholasville was expanding with the growth of Lexington. A new subdivision went up south of town. John casually suggested David purchase one of the new houses. "We can give you a very low rate of interest on a loan. After all, it won't be long before you take my place as President."

Surprised, David looked up from his paperwork. "I have been considering purchasing one those houses, but you will be President a long time."

"You know I will be sixty-six in March and the wife wants to do some traveling. She keeps talking about a trip to England, seeing some of the live shows, Big Ben, and traveling by train up to Paris, France to visit the Louvre, the Eiffel Tower, and the Tomb of Napoléon."

"Why John, I did not know you like to travel."

"I don't, but the missus does. It is all she can talk about–retiring and traveling. I feel I owe it to her. She has put up with me all these years. I think I could enjoy it."

"Well, I'm sure you would."

"It may be soon."

"This bank has really grown under your leadership," said David.

"It was your idea to place a branch in Lexington. That has really helped the bank. It was you that suggested painting this old structure and putting in a bigger vault, printing and mailing out statements, and starting children's accounts. The growth we have seen is largely due to your foresight and recommendations."

David dropped his head, embarrassed. "Yes, but you convinced the Trustees to do all these things. They would not have followed my suggestions if it had not been for you selling the ideas."

"I'm not convinced of that. If I stepped out tomorrow, you could step right in. You know as much about banking as I do now."

Three years later, on a trip to London, their fourth trip abroad, in a hotel room, John died in his sleep. David received a frantic phone call from John's wife Heather announcing his passing. Assuring David of how much

John thought of him, she went on and on. "I just don't know what I am going to do. How will I get his body home, David?"

"Do you have the money for the arrangements to get John home?"

"Yes, I think so!"

"Check on that and let me know."

"Thank you! I will make preparations tomorrow for myself and the children to book passage on one of the steamers."

"Let me know, Heather, and I will make arrangement for passage of John's body. John can be buried in a London cemetery, or he can be transported back home."

Heather contacted the pastor of Chandler Baptist Church, where they attended when visiting London, requesting prayer for the family. Arrangements were made for a London burial right next to the church. It would be a long trip home. It rained throughout the whole day of the funeral. The pastor preached a short fifteen-minute message using the text of Psalm 23, emphasizing that the Shepherd knew His sheep and assuring the people that gathered before the grave that His sheep knew the Shepherd.

A simple headstone read.

John Martin,
faithful husband, loyal friend,
servant of God.

David hung the phone up and was still processing the call, when the little bell on the door rang as Frank Thornton entered. He went straight to David's desk. "Mr. Matthews," he began. David held up a hand, "It is David. I am much younger than you. What can I help you with today Frank?"

Clearing his throat, "Well David, I need a new tractor and I was wondering if I could finance it through the bank?"

"What type of tractor are you looking at?"

"A John Deere," he said as if there was no other brand. "Bill Markham has one and he is really happy with it."

"You always have a fine crop, and I am sure we can work something out. Make the arrangements for what you want, and we will draw up the papers for the purchase."

"That was easy!"

"You are a good customer Frank, and you have been with us here at the bank for a long time," David replied, standing and shaking his hand.

Hardly had Frank left when Helen Smith came through the door in a huff. "David, I have made a big mistake on my checking account. It looks like I will overdraw $8.00 before I get my next check. Since, my Marvin passed away I just have a hard time making it."

"Not to worry Helen, I will take care of it. I can hold the overdrawn check for a few extra days. You will not overdraw." She stood, straightened her hat and thanked him profusely.

David left the bank early that morning to take his carriage to Ben's blacksmith shop to get a cracked spoke replaced. As soon as he walked into the shop he sensed something was wrong. Ben ran the shop along with his elderly father. He seemed troubled and was having a hard time concentrating.

"David, you are just the person I need to talk to. Let's go into my office."

David followed him into the shabby office wondering what grave thing he had to tell him. *Maybe he had some terrible disease, or maybe one of his children was diagnosed with some rare form of illness. Was he in financial trouble? Was it some spiritual problem?* He and his family had attended Nicholasville Baptist Church where David was occasionally a deacon.

Ben closed the door, locking it behind him. He motioned toward a chair for David to be seated. He remained standing for a few moments. "I have a big problem, David. My wife came in the other night and told me that she didn't love me anymore and wanted a divorce. People say she has been going with Mary Clarkson to bars a couple of times a week to hear country bands play, but I think there is more to it–nothing between her and Mary, but perhaps meeting other men. I just do not know what to do." Sitting there, rocking back and forth, he bore his soul. "Mary Clarkson is divorced and very wealthy. She paid for them to go to Nashville for two weekends to (holding up his fingers in a quotation sign), 'hear famous bands play.'"

"I sensed something was wrong when I entered the garage. This is troubling Ben."

"We have been married eleven years. I thought we had a near perfect marriage. We have a daughter that's nine years old and a son that is six, in the first grade. She wants me to move out of the house into an apartment. I do all the cooking at home, keep up the laundry, and help the kids with their studies. I think I am a good husband. What am I going to do?" he groaned, placing his head in his hands.

Just then, his dad knocked on the door. "You have a customer's son that wants you to give him an estimate on his carriage repair."

"I can't talk to him right now, Dad. You have done this hundreds of times before. Give him a figure and I will make it work, or ask if he can come back this afternoon or tomorrow."

"All right!

Loud cursing filled the air. "If your son isn't interested in my business, I will take it somewhere else." David stood up. "I can wait until you give him an estimate."

"No, sit down, David. I need to talk to you. Besides, there is no one else for twenty-five miles that does blacksmith work. I am good at what I do, and he knows it. Anyway, Jim is too tight to go anywhere else. He knows I am more reasonable than the blacksmith in Lexington. After he cools off, he will be back this afternoon. He has a short fuse, but he gets over his mad spells quickly," Ben said, laughing.

"I have heard your story a couple of times before. There was a deacon in our church, I can't say who, that began to sob uncontrollably one night in a deacon's meeting.

His wife essentially told him the same thing. It has been six or seven years ago. They had four children, two of them at University."

"What did he do? What happened?"

"They went for counseling with the Pastor a couple of times; then they didn't come back. Later, it was said that she had an emotional problem of some type and that she was involved in some sort of extramarital affair."

"I don't think that is the case, yet, with Brenda; however, if she keeps going to the bars for whatever reason she is risking meeting someone. What do you think I should do? Do you think I should move into an apartment and let her do the cooking and laundry to see what living alone is all about?"

"I am not a counselor, but I don't think you ought to move out of the house. Who keeps the kids when she is gone to work? The kids must ask where their Mom is when she is gone?"

"My Mom keeps them after school when she is out of town. Oh, and she wants total custody of the children, but that is never going to happen," he declared firmly. "No matter what happens, she is not taking our children away from me."

"First, I think you ought to see if she was willing to go with you to a Christian counselor to see if you can get things worked out. In the meantime, you need to get yourself into a church."

"I have already suggested that, but she says we don't need a counselor. Her mind is made up."

"Let's put this in the Lord's hand right now. May I pray with you?"

"Certainly, please do."

> *"Lord, eternal God, we come to you right now on behalf of Ben and Brenda's marriage. You are our great Healer and Helper. Only you can repair this broken marriage. We know that you do not override human will, but we ask that you will touch Brenda's heart and make her aware of what she is doing to her family. Put in her path obstacles to continued actions that hurt this relationship. Rekindle her love for Ben. Put a hedge around Ben to keep him from making foolish choices and actions. In the Name that is above every name Our Lord and Savior Jesus Christ, we pray."*

Over the next month David and Sarah prayed for the marriage and reconciliation of the couple. David checked in at the business and asked, "How are things going?" whenever Cecil's dad or customers were not around.

"Well, I retained a lawyer and moved into an apartment. I go each day after work to see the children and spend time with them. She acts like I am not even there. The children keep asking why I am not there all the time. I just tell them that Mommy and Daddy have some things to work out. I am praying every night and day that she will get over this. I have started going to a Nazarene Chapel on most Sundays. I can't bear going to your church and people asking where my wife is."

Three weeks later, Ben stopped by the bank and pulled David aside. "Brenda is back to her old self. I have moved back in and she seems past whatever was going on in her life before. You will be seeing us in church Sunday. Things are not perfect, but they are eighty percent better and she isn't going out at nights and on the weekends."

"I will be looking for you and Brenda on Sunday. Sarah and I will save you a seat beside us. This is such an answer to prayer. Let's give God the glory right now."

"Thank you Heavenly Father for the healing power of Your Holy Spirit. We give you all the glory for working in this marriage. You are truly the Great Physician. In Jesus Name we pray. Amen!"

CHAPTER THIRTEEN

S ATURDAY, APRIL 8, 1922, was one of the last big furniture sales that David and Henry attended together. It was the South Union Shaker furniture auction. Hundreds of people attended. Automobiles lined the main road before the Centre House. Many were there for the social reasons and others to purchase some of the Shaker items. David had his own wagon and team by now, but Henry brought his in case David over-bought, which he did. He was particularly interested in damaged pieces he could repair before selling. Those were limited but sold cheaply when brought up for sale. However, he bought several fine pieces that were in perfect shape. Of course, he had to pay through the nose for some of the better items.

He was selling Shaker pieces almost weekly from his little barn. Customers were often waiting at his front door when he arrived home from work. The Shakers were known for their fine craftsmanship of simple pieces. None of these real craftsmen were living at Pleasant Hill or South Union. They had died off in the years before the closing of the Communities.

At 10:30 sharp the first auctioneer took the stand. The crowd began to quiet down. All the household and kitchen articles were sold first. The bill of sale listed many of the items: chest of drawers, tables both large and small, twin beds, wardrobes, cupboards, straight-back chairs, feather beds, carpets, bed clothes, and other articles too numerous to mention. Many were walnut, cherry, or oak, most of which were made from lumber cut on the Shaker property. Several items were advertised as 100 years old.

The terms were cash with no reserves and open bidding only. Transportation was furnished to and from the sale at the railroad station where there was adequate parking.

Five months later, on September 27, the same auctioneer, Colonel W.A. Holeman, stood before a large crowd to offer for sale the buildings and the land. Local churchwomen provided home cooked food for sale. Farm machinery, some Shaker furniture, cattle, and buildings were sold to an investment firm. Although the furniture for sale was limited, David and Henry were there. Many in the crowd recognize the two young men from previous sales and resigned to the fact they would not be getting any bargains.

Early in the auction a round table with six chairs came up for sale. It looked like it had been handled rather roughly or even stored for a long while. The chairs had a couple support rods broken. Perhaps a child may have stood up on them. It was made of hard wood hickory. The rods would be easily replaced in David's shop.

"Here we have this fine table with six chairs. Who will start the bidding at $25.00?"

"I'll start the bidding at $15.00. There is damage on the chairs," said a prominent local lawyer.

"Fifteen dollars. Well, that is a place to begin," said the auctioneer.

"I'll give you $21. 35," said David.

People in the crowd laughed at the unusual bid. David just smiled.

"I'll give you $23.51," called another man now on his feet bidding, his wife pulling him down by his coat. Laughter again broke out from the crowd, but he remained standing as he bid.

The auctioneer paused. "Now gentlemen this is far too little money for this beautiful hand-crafted Shaker set. Let's get serious."

"I am serious," said the man, "I want that table and chairs." By now he was looking straight at David.

"I want it too! Sir, do you want it more than I do?" David was now standing smiling at the man. The crowd was now going wild, laughing and pointing at the two.

"I appreciate this table and chairs. What interest do you have in them?"

"Nothing more than the fact I was raised in a Shaker Village and ate around a table like this every day." The crowd howled clapping their hands.

"Let the young man have it," called a strong voice from the back of the room.

"I'll give you," addressing the auctioneer, "$30.00 and it is my final bid," said the man from New York, his wife still tugging on his coattail.

"I'll raise the bid to $35.00 and that may not be my final offer." David sat down and the crowd chanted, "Let the Shaker have it."

Standing again, David raised his hand to quiet the crowd. "I was raised at Pleasant Hill Village, but I never signed the Covenant to become a Shaker. I fell in love and got married." The crowd grew quiet. "Let me say that I am a Baptist now, but I have great respect for the Shakers," glancing over at Sister Mary Settles who was visiting the auction. She was enjoying the banter back and forth; as she hobbled to her feet, the crowd grew quiet. "I am a Shaker and I knew this boy. He is a fine young man." She bowed as a roar of applause again filled the air as she sat down.

"Going for $35.00 once, going twice, gone," proclaimed the auctioneer.

While they were taking a rest on the way home Henry said, "I sure thought that gentlemen from New York was going to win the bid on that table and chairs, but you persevered to the end."

"Yes, I thought he would split his pants when I bid $35.00 for the set. I told him later if he really wanted the table and chairs I would let him have it for twice the amount I paid. No, I am joking; I told him if he really wanted the set that he could have it for what I paid for it. Actually, I wanted to keep it, repair it, and refinish it. I think it will fit nicely in our dining room."

"What will Sarah think of you bringing in all these remembrances of the past?"

"Oh, she will like it, or we won't keep it. She knows how much I appreciate the Shakers for taking me in and giving me a good work ethic. After all, we would have never met had it not been for the Shakers."

"I guess so. I hadn't thought about that," said Henry, climbing back into his wagon and gently cracking the whip over the horse's back. "Getty-up, Josephine."

David pulled his father's watch from his pocket. It was four o'clock. "It should take us about two hours to get home. Just in time for supper," called David from his wagon. It was always breakfast, dinner, and supper, a fall back on their Shaker upbringing, never breakfast, lunch and dinner,

They sang Christian hymns and talked about the Village—Henry almost drowning at the pond, long talks at night discussing Shaker beliefs, putting the frog in Henry's bed, joining the Union forces, Randall Blevins becoming David's roommate and leading him to Christ, the report of Henry's death and the part that the watch played in his return, Henry's becoming a medic, shooting the Confederate soldier, and David slipping out at night to visit Sarah at the Landing.

Almost home, just outside Bardstown, the back wheel on the passenger's side gave away. Henry pulled to a stop. "I knew I should have replaced that wheel before we left.

I could see that it was weak. Good thing I have a spare, so let's get to changing it."

The first problem was unloading the furniture off of the wagon in order to get to the extra wheel. Then there was the problem of propping the bed up to get the wheel off the axel. Fortunately, there was a creek nearby where they retrieved enough rock to support the bed. It took two hours and fifteen minutes to repair the wagon and get the furniture reloaded.

"I am really sorry about this," said David.

"It is not your fault. I should have taken care of that wheel when I first noticed it."

"I have got to get a larger wagon, so I don't put you out with these trips."

"Are you serious? These trips are a blast. I wouldn't miss an auction for anything."

At eleven o'clock they pulled up to the building where David had his shop. It took an hour longer to unload the items. "Well, this is going to be a late supper. I am sure Sarah has it in the oven. Why, don't you eat with us before you go?"

"David, I had better get home. Elizabeth will be worried about us, but thanks anyway. And, I have hospital calls in Lexington early tomorrow morning."

Henry pulled out, tapping Josephine on the back; little did David know that it would be their last big trip together. A month later while visiting the Psychiatric Ward of the Lexington Hospital, a psychotic war soldier thought Henry was the enemy and stabbed him in the chest. Henry almost died and would have had it not been for an assistant restraining the soldier to keep him from stabbing him again.

David stood by his hospital bed every day after work. "Are you going to be all right?"

"Of course I am going to be all right. When is our next auction?" Over the next few weeks Henry finally recovered and was back to work.

"The next auction is a small one that will have only a couple of Shaker pieces, but Saturday, weather permitting.

It was hog-killing time at the Miles farm. Each year Thomas purchased four piglets from his neighbor George Howlett, a local farmer, feeding them until butchering time, one for David's family, one for Billy's family, and two for him and Francis. It was a festive time for the families. Frances kept the children, all five of them, feeding them snacks and playing games with them at home. Martha, Billy's wife, and Sarah help the men scrap the hair from the freshly slaughtered hogs, lying on a cleaning table.

Everything was processed except the honk. The head, tail, entrails, and feet were given to a poor family across the river. Occasionally, Thomas would keep a hog's head for the brains, which were served up for breakfast with fresh eggs from the chicken house. Hams and shoulders of the hog were dry rubbed with a mixture of salt, paprika, a little sugar, and a few other spices, wrapped in paper, and covered in cloth to be hung up in the meat house to cure until their time to be eaten. Ideally, these parts of the hog hung in the meat house for at least a year to cure.

Other parts of the hog such as racks of ribs, slabs of bacon, and pork chops were smoked. After being rubbed down with salt they were hung in the special built smokehouse where smoke was channeled from the outside to the inside from a large fire pit. After at least five or six days, the meat was taken down and cut up. Any meat left was wrapped in cloth and then rehung.

Country pork sausages are made from parts that are leftover after the larger parts have been processed, although most any part of the hog may be used for sausage. Blends of different spices such as pepper, sage, and coriander are mixed with the meat before being ground and placed in cloth bags. Some of the fat of the hog is mixed with leaner cuts, but most of it is used for rendering lard to cook with. Chunks of fat connected to carefully cleaned skin are boiled in a large iron kettle over an open fire. Once the fat is boiled into lard, the skin, or cracklings, that are left are separated to be pressed for any additional lard, leaving the skins that are left to be made into cracklings–a delicious for snacks or mixed in corn bread.

Neighbors helped neighbors at hog killing time in order to process the meat more quickly. At the end of the day, tired workers often enjoyed a supper of fresh pork meat. The fresh meat hung in the smokehouse that was secured by lock to keep thieves from stealing it. After a proper time of curing, the meat was divided to family members. Butchering hogs was a tiresome process, but it was also a festive time at the Miles household.

CHAPTER FOURTEEN

D AVID WAS SITTING at his desk thinking about a recent loan he had made to Jeremiah Johnson, pastor of the African American Baptist Church, when the little brass bell over the door tingled. It was clearly closing time and he had locked the door after the last customer. Someone was trying to get in. He looked up at the old Regular Clock on the wall behind the President's desk. The other workers had gone home leaving him alone in the bank. He wondered *who could that be at this late hour* as he stood up from his desk to unlock the door. Virginia Walters, wife of local Judge Sidney Walters, walked in chatting as the door opened, "Sorry, to come so late, but Sidney wanted me to drop these checks off for deposit," she said as she slid her arm through David's to be escorted to the teller window. Surprised, David took her to the window, slipping his arm from hers as he stepped aside to go to the back of the counter.

"Sidney does not like to keep money at home; we have been robbed twice you know."

"Actually, I had not heard that."

She shoved the pile of checks through the iron frame and laid her hand upon David's as he reached to take the items. David flushed a little and smiled thinking it was only an accident, but she lingered. He moved the pile of checks from under his hand and began to total them up.

Clearly flustered, he kept hitting the wrong keys on the new Don E Felt adding machine, having to start over.

"I like the way you comb your handsome head of hair straight back" Virginia commented, smiling.

Ignoring the comment, David continued to add up the checks.

"You know Sidney is gone so much of the time that it may be necessary to come by the house sometime and pick the deposits up."

"I suppose Sarah and I could do that if it ever became necessary. I am sure Sarah would come with me."

Nervously, he finished the total twice and quickly shoved the receipt under the iron frame. "That should take care of everything, Mrs. Walters."

"Well, aren't you going to walk me to the door?"

"No, I will finish up here and lock the door when I leave. I am sure Sarah is wondering why I am late."

Sauntering to the door, she turned, "It was so nice to see you today, David."

"Thank you for your business, Mrs. Walters."

David was visibly shaken that sweat was beading up on his forehead. His hand was trembling as he picked up the checks and headed to the vault. Try as he did, he kept fumbling with the combination to open the safe. Finally, it clicked open. He shoved the checks into a basket on the wall and closed the large, heavy iron door as rapidly as possible.

Looking around to make sure that she had gone, he placed the key in the old brass lock and headed down the street to his beloved Sarah. Ruth was playing in the yard with a friend when she saw her father come through the wrought iron gate. Running to him, she hugged him and introduced her new friend Heather. Her family had just moved to Nicholasville from Tennessee; her father was the new plant manager of the hemp factory at the east end of town.

"Heather, we are members of the First Baptist Church," said David, "and if your family does not have a church home, we would love to have your family as our guests on Sunday."

"Thank you, Mr. Matthews, but we are Presbyterians," replied Heather.

"Well, they have built a fine, new Presbyterian Church up on 101 North Street. They have a great pastor too."

Sarah was standing at the door smiling. David rushed up to her and gave her a big hug, holding her tight for the longest time.

"Well, what is the occasion?"

"Just to let you know how much I love you."

"Thank you, I love you too. You're a little late and dinner is ready"

"Yes, I got held up at the last minute by a customer."

After a fine dinner of roast lamb, potatoes, carrots, and onions, David excused himself to go back to the bank and finish up some loan applications.

"David, you are having to put in a lot of late hours lately."

"Yes, we have been flooded with loan applications and there are new government guidelines that we have to comply with."

As he poured over the new restrictions, the phone rang. It was Virginia Walters. "I was walking by the bank and I saw that you are working late. I would like to come in and talk to you. Sidney is on a trip to Cincinnati, and I am very lonely."

"Mrs. Walters, I am knee deep in paperwork, and it would not be proper for you to do so at such a late hour. The bank is closed. If you have a business matter you might come by and talk with Marjorie Kennedy, one of our bright new employees. She transferred from our new office in Lexington last month."

"I want to talk to you David."

Ignoring her direct request David suggested she and Mr. Walters make an appointment for an after-hours meeting. "I am sorry, but I have to get back to my work here."

"David, I am in love with you," she said frankly.

"Mrs. Walters, I am going to hang up and forget that you said that." As he hung up, he heard soft crying on the other end.

The next day he pulled Matthew Parker, a long- time teller at the bank, aside and told him what had happened. "That is very troublesome. I know that Sidney is gone a lot."

"If she comes in, I want you or Marjorie Kennedy to deal with her. Marjorie need not know about this conversation, and Matt, you must not leave me at the bank alone. Someone must be here with me, preferable a male employee."

"I totally understand. I suppose I need to be here when you work late at night."

"I am just about finished with the new requirements, but if you could be here the next couple of nights, I would appreciate it."

"Of course. I think that is best."

When David returned home that evening, he saw a letter, addressed to Sarah, opened on the hall table. "I wasn't going to show you this, but we need to talk."

"Yes, we do." David picked the brief note up and began to read it. It was from Virginia Walters.

> *Sarah, I think you need to know that I have been seeing your husband at the bank after hours. He has shown interest in me. I have fallen in love with him and he with me.*
>
> *Virginia Walters*

"She has lost her mind." David shared what had happened at the bank and assured Sarah that he had ignored her advances.

"I know, darling. I just felt I should show the note to you. I trust you implicitly. Virginia is a very troubled lady."

"It is as if she wanted to be found out. I am going to show this note to Judge Walters tomorrow. This has got to end."

David stood nervously before Judge Walter's secretary requesting to see him.

"He has a hearing at two o'clock and has appointments until then. What about tomorrow around one o'clock?"

"No," David said sternly, "I must see him immediately." He was shaking, and the secretary saw his urgency. She stood up and walked to the door.

"Let, me speak to him and see if we can work you in this morning." She was now standing at his door.

"Have a seat Mr. Matthews, and I will check with the Judge. I will tell him it is very important."

David had hardly seated himself when the Judge appeared at the door and motioned him to come in.

"I am glad to see you this morning, Judge. I have been wanting to talk with you," he stated, extending his hand. "I don't know how to begin. Maybe this note from Mrs. Walters to my wife will reveal why I am here. Judge, I have no interest in your wife. I am happily married…" Judge Walters raised his hand as he read the note.

"I am sure you have done nothing improper David. Virginia is having some serious problems."

David sat back relieved as the Judge looked out the window. When he turned back around, tears had filled his eyes. "I have to get her help. This is not the first time that this has happened. She became infatuated with the milkman. He ended up moving to another town."

"I hope this won't affect your relationship with the bank. We value you as an important customer."

"No, it won't. You need not be concerned with that," he said, standing. "I have an appointment with the Mayor. I will take care of this when I get home tonight."

"Sir, if I may be so bold as to say this..."

"Yes, go ahead, David."

"Maybe if you took her with you on your trips out of town?"

"That is a good suggestion and I will consider it, but Virginia needs professional help," he replied as he arose from his desk and moved to the door.

"Yes, sir. Thank you for understanding."

"I am sorry, you and your dear wife had to go through this," he apoligzed, opening door.

David drew a sigh of relief as he greeted the Mayor before leaving.

Virginia Walters entered the Saint Joseph Hospital psychiatry ward where she was treated for several months. She never went to David's desk again until one day she said in passing, "I am very sorry," going straight to Marjorie Kennedy's window. David smiled, nodding without verbal response.

CHAPTER FIFTEEN

HENRY LINGERED AS the last customer left the bank. David locked the door.

"There is a musical about a romance that that has as its setting in a Shaker Village. It is called *Amor, or the Pretty Shakeress*. It is a musical comedy that is being performed by a Harrodsburg group at the Pioneer Memorial Park Theater tomorrow night. I thought you and Sarah might like to accompany Elizabeth and me to see it. I have two extra tickets."

"Sounds great! Let me check with Sarah to see if we have any plans."

"You can let us know tonight at supper. Had you forgotten that you are to eat with us?"

"Actually, I had, but I am sure that Sarah has not."

The performance was filled with hymns, customs, and religious dances of the Shakers. The play drew upon the Shaker restrictions of the Village against romantic activity. The younger Shakers ignored the rules and got together at times. It was a hilarious presentation of the spiritual marriage, taught by the Shakers, with the carnal marriage of the flesh.

On the way home, the two couples discussed the humorous parts of the play; fresh in all their minds, however, was the fact that the Shakers were a dying sect–their buildings crumbling and those left were trying to provide for themselves by selling off parts of land and auctioning off the furniture left in the empty buildings. Ultimately, the Shaker land on both sides of the river was sold.

Things were no better at the Logan County South Union Village, located in Auburn, Kentucky. The Village was founded in 1807 with numerous buildings that were ultimately reduced to a forty-room Centre House, which serves as a museum today. The building is filled with original furnishings revealing Shaker workmanship.

On April 30, 1871, the Village experienced a terrible windstorm of hail and rain, blowing two of the chimneys off the West Family house, tearing shingles off the barn, and destroying lots of fruit trees. The couples talked about the devastation of the storm, which had also damaged houses and businesses in Nicholasville and Harrodsburg.

The next day, Saturday, Shaker Village was having a big furniture sale and David and Henry planned to be there. David was already buying up Shaker pieces for his antique store. It began with a large shed in the back of his house. He saw the value in the items that would no longer be produced. The auction terms had just been explained, sales were final, it was up to the buyer to examine and note flaws. It was a cash only sale.

Mary Settles was present, dressed in her white starched bonnet, blue Shaker blouse, white dress, and worn Shaker shoes. She had come to Shaker Village when her husband abandoned her after the birth of their second child. Her own mother had died in childbirth, and Mary was told that she could not have any more children. Her husband, who wanted a big family of ten children, asked her for a divorce.

Abandoned Mary and her two children came to Shaker Village, where she came to embrace the Shaker religion. Having previously been a teacher in the Louisville Public School system, she became a teacher at the Village for many years.

In September 1910, Shaker Village at Pleasant Hill closed its doors. The twelve remaining members, under the guidance of William F. Pennebaker, deeded the final 1,800 acres of land to a local merchant by the name of George Bohon, of Harrodsburg, with the understanding that all their needs would be provided for until death. The remaining twelve Shakers signed the agreement. Bohon did likewise, and later deeded 650 acres of land back to Dr. W. F. Pennebaker for him and his family. Upon Pennebaker's death, the land was deeded for the establishment of the Penne-baker Home for Girls.

Sister Mary Settles, as she was fondly referred to, became the last living Shaker at Pleasant Hill, preceded in death by all other leaders in the Village. However, she was not the last Shaker in Kentucky to die. Previously, Annie Farmer and her mother Alice Mason, both Shakers, moved to Louisville. Her mother preceded her in death, but Annie died in 1942 and was buried in the Evergreen Cemetery in Louisville.

On March 29, 1923, Mary Clark Carmichael Settles died at the Centre Family House at the age of 86. She was buried in the small Shaker cemetery at Pleasant Hill. An anonymous person had cleared the little graveyard of all weeds.

A choir from the African Methodist Church sang a familiar Shaker funeral hymn:

> *"Our sister's gone, she is no more,*
> *She quit our coast, she's left our shore,*
> *She's burst the bonds of mortal clay,*
> *The spirit's fled and soars away."*

The Pastor of the Church reminded the few that had gathered from Harrodsburg, including merchant George Bohon and two businessmen from Louisville, of Mary Settles faithfulness and devout leadership in the Shaker community as an Elderess and teacher. He further noted that in her last years she had been a champion for the Women's Suffrage movement, voting for the first time in 1920. He was careful not to call her a Christian in the traditional sense but noted that she was a good person of devout Shaker beliefs. He was short, but kind in his remarks. There were no flowers to be laid on her grave.

Before he said the benediction, he asked if anyone there had anything to say. David stepped forward and said, "Years ago, Dr. Devoe and I were brought to Pleasant Hill from an orphanage in New Orleans by Deacon Micajah Burnett when we were twelve years old. Sister Mary Settles was very sensitive to our uncertainty as to what to expect. She showed us our room and talked about how pleased they were to have us. She promised that we would eat well, work hard, and learn a trade." David stepped back. No one else had anything to say so the Pastor gave the benediction in which he thanked God for His mercy and forgiveness through the cross and the resurrection. An unknown man, perhaps the one that cleaned the graveyard off, remained to cover the wooden casket as the others dismissed, returning to their respective homes.

David hesitated while everyone but he, Henry, and the man were left at the grave. "Is someone paying for your services?" asked David.

The man smiled, "In fact, the casket and my services were paid for by Miss. Settles over the past two years. She knew she was nearing the end of her journey, as she put it, and started paying on the expenses of her burial. I work for the Baker Funeral Home in Harrodsburg. Thank you for asking."

On her tombstone, according to Shaker tradition, were her initials M.S., except for Mother Ann Lee, founder of the American Shakers, that read, "Mother Ann Lee, born in Manchester, England February 29, 1736, died in Watervliet, N.Y. September 8, 1784." David and Henry stood at the gravesite as her lifeless body was lowered into the grave. Both men wept quietly.

Over the next fifty years, the once beautiful buildings experienced continued decay. Weeds covered the small graveyard, a sign of the end of Shakerism at Pleasant Hill. Between the closing of the village and the beginning of their restoration in 1961, some of the buildings were used for utilitarian purposes. The meetinghouse became a car garage. It's floor, built to bear the weight of a hundred or more dancing Shakers, supported the less heavy automobiles of that time for repairs. The meetinghouse, built in 1820 under the design and oversight of Micajah Burnett, sixty feet long and forty-four feet wide, became the Shakertown Baptist Church for several years. After the purchase of the village by a group of business-people, the church continued to function until an agreement was reached between the owners of the other buildings and the church to build a new church and parsonage on an outside piece of property a mile away. A tearoom occupied one of the buildings for a short time. The carpenter's shop, which later became a general store, was later restored as the broom workshop. The deacon's shop became a gas filling station. Sharecroppers occupied the empty buildings at different times, leaving them in worst conditions than when they came. The Trustee Office was turned into a restaurant and remains so today.

After several failed efforts to restore and preserve Pleasant Hill, in 1961, a private nonprofit group of merchants and business people from the surrounding areas formed "Shaker Village of Pleasant Hill." It was not until 1965, with the restoring of the main road to the Village, that the restoration begun. It was a gigantic undertaking. Blood, sweat, and tears went into restoring the historic property. Without the assistance of government funds or grants, a small fee was charged to view the restored community, which was not enough to sustain costs of its upkeep. Craft shops were opened to support the effort along with private sacrificial gifts. In addition, the Federal Economic Development Administration loaned the group $2 million dollars to help in the project. Living quarters were developed that may be rented, adding to the support of the Village.

Today, thirty-four beautifully restored buildings and farmland grace the 2,700 acres. Among them is the restaurant that produces delicious food from the original recipes of the Shakers. Fine period furniture fills the family quarters where people visiting can view how the Shakers lived and flourished in the 1800s.

Neither David nor Henry lived to see the restoration of the main buildings of Pleasant Hill. David died of polycystic kidney disease at the age of seventy. Two years later, at seventy-two, Sarah passed over Jordan. Their youngest child Ruth and Benjamin, her older brother, sold, along with the house, the Shaker antique business at auction. Henry practiced medicine until he died of old age at eighty-three. Previously, Randell Blevins retired as Editor of the Cleveland newspaper and died in his sleep three days later at the age of ninety-one.

Only two Shakers remain of the religious sect The United Society of Christ's Second Appearing. They live at Sabbath Day Lake Shaker Community in New Gloucester, Maine. There have been those that considered joining the Shakers there but later left the community for different reasons. Some could not bear the rigors of a hard labor that the Shaker life required. Others could not live the celibate life of a Shaker. The community is no longer open to converts.

Until recently, there were four living Shakers. One of those is Wayne Smith that left the community at forty-nine years of age after living there for several years. Smith became romantically involved with a female newspaper reporter that came to the Village to do an article on the Shakers and later married her. Francis Carr, a long time member, recently died at the age of eighty-nine. There only remain two members today. Fifty-eight year old Arnold Hadd grew up in western Massachusetts and joined the Shakers around twenty-one years of age. Hadd tends the 1,800+ acre farm where he raises beef cattle and fruit trees, particularly apple trees. The other remaining member is seventy-eight-year-old June Carpenter. They live communally celibate lives at the Gloucester, Maine Village, the only remaining active Shaker Community still in existence of the eighteen once established across the United States.

CPSIA information can be obtained
at www.ICGtesting.com
Printed in the USA
BVHW031603161219
566814BV00006B/70/P